"Blake?" Her voice was hoarse.

She thought she was reading the signs right, that he'd finally noticed she was a woman. But she was afraid to make any moves without knowing for sure. "Are you hungry for the cheeseburger? Or...me?"

His gaze shot to hers. "What cheeseburger?"

"Oh, thank God," she whispered, just before he swooped down and pressed his lips to hers.

They were both gasping for air when he broke the kiss.

"Donna?"

The sound of her name whispered in husky, deep tones next to her ear sent shivers up her spine.

"I want to feel your skin against mine," she whispered. "You have too many clothes on."

He swallowed and rested his forehead against hers. "Are you sure you want this?"

Finally, finally, he was as hungry for her as she'd been for him for so very, very long.

"If you stop right now, I'm going to shoot you. How's that for being sure?"

SWAT STANDOFF

———

LENA DIAZ

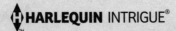

This story is dedicated to the *Tennessee Takedown* readers who demanded that I make it a series. I've absolutely *loved* writing these stories about the Destiny, Tennessee, SWAT team. I hope readers love *SWAT Standoff*, the exciting conclusion to this thrilling ride.

ISBN-13: 978-1-335-63927-1

SWAT Standoff

Copyright © 2018 by Lena Diaz

PLEASE RECYCLE
THIS PRODUCT IS RECYCLABLE

Recycling programs for this product may not exist in your area.

For questions and comments about the quality of this book, please contact us at CustomerService@Harlequin.com.

Printed in U.S.A.

HARLEQUIN®
www.Harlequin.com

Lena Diaz was born in Kentucky and has also lived in California, Louisiana and Florida, where she now resides with her husband and two children. Before becoming a romantic suspense author, she was a computer programmer. A Romance Writers of America Golden Heart® Award finalist, she has also won the prestigious Daphne du Maurier Award for Excellence in Mystery/Suspense. To get the latest news about Lena, please visit her website, lenadiaz.com.

Books by Lena Diaz

Harlequin Intrigue

Tennessee SWAT

Mountain Witness
Secret Stalker
Stranded with the Detective
SWAT Standoff

Marshland Justice

Missing in the Glades
Arresting Developments
Deep Cover Detective
Hostage Negotiation

The Marshal's Witness
Explosive Attraction
Undercover Twin
Tennessee Takedown
The Bodyguard

Visit the Author Profile page at Harlequin.com.

CAST OF CHARACTERS

Blake Sullivan—The newest member of the Destiny, Tennessee, SWAT team is struggling to fit in. If he doesn't figure it out soon, the fate of the entire team could hang in the balance.

Donna Waters—Tasked with helping fellow SWAT officer Blake learn the ropes, her skills will be stretched to the limit when it's just her and Blake who have to save the rest of the team.

Richard Grant—This FBI supervisory special agent is supposed to investigate a murder and determine what happened to the SWAT team. But does he really want to help? Or is he putting up roadblocks to stall the investigation?

Colin Lopez—Grant's right-hand agent. But why is he slipping off to Knoxville every day? Could he be the one behind what's happened to the SWAT team?

Rodney Lynch—When Blake and Donna need insider information, they turn to this Destiny police officer. Is he feeding them valuable information or sending them on a wild-goose chase?

Tim Nealy—Hired to help with a SWAT team exercise, his claims cause severe problems between the FBI and Blake. Is he trying to sabotage the investigation?

Stacy Bell—Another one of Grant's agents, she seems sympathetic to the SWAT situation. But her reasons for being in Destiny may be more complicated than anyone realizes.

Sanchez—This alleged Colombian drug lord keeps coming up as each thread is pulled in the investigation. He may be critical to finding out who's really behind what happened.

Chapter One

SWAT Officer Blake Sullivan crouched behind some honeysuckle-vine-covered logs and peered at the weathered gray barn through his rifle scope. His target was little more than a shadow in the second-story window that had probably lost its glass long before Blake was born. How the suspect had managed to get up that high without crashing through the rotten stairs or floorboards was a mystery. The dilapidated building should have collapsed long ago in the violent winds that sometimes blew down from the nearby Smoky Mountains. Blake imagined the only reason that it hadn't fallen down yet was that it was sheltered from the elements by a thick stand of Tennessee sugar maples and white flowering dogwoods.

With the early morning sun slanting through the trees behind him, and a lull in the light spring breeze that had been blowing moments before, conditions were perfect to take the shot.

He eased his finger from the cold frame of his rifle to the smooth, welcoming cradle of the trigger.

Two chirps followed by a high-pitched whistle sounded off to his left. It sounded just like a bobwhite bird, common here at Hawkins Ridge and Tennessee in general. But Blake knew better. That was the SWAT team leader, Dillon Gray, signaling him. But if Blake looked away, he might lose the perpetrator. Dillon would have to wait.

Ignoring a second, more insistent whistle, he edged the barrel of the rifle down a fraction, exhaled slowly and squeezed.

Pop.

Red bloomed across the suspect's chest. He cartwheeled backward, disappearing from sight.

Blake grinned. One down; one to go. Now he could see what Dillon wanted.

He looked over his left shoulder. The team leader stood a good twenty yards away, talking to Donna Waters, the only female member of their team. Dressed in green camouflage, they both would've completely blended into their surroundings if it wasn't for the white S-W-A-T letters across Dillon's back. Neither of them seemed to notice Blake. Whatever Dillon had wanted earlier must not have been that important.

Blake turned his attention back to the barn.

Had the suspects split up? Initially, they'd worked as a team, staying close together. If they stuck to that plan, the second one had to be somewhere close by.

Nearly a full minute later, his patience was rewarded. A dark shadow moved near some trees to the right of the building. The man furtively looked around as if to see whether anyone had spotted him. Destiny, Tennessee's entire seven-member SWAT team, plus their chief, was out here somewhere. Correction, *six*-member team, now that Colby had taken a new job a couple hours' drive from Blount County.

Blake glanced back to signal Dillon and Donna. But, either they were blending in with the trees so well that he couldn't see them now, or they were gone. He considered radioing the team to let them know he'd gotten one of the suspects and had eyes on the second. But he worried there might be static or that the sound of his voice would spook his prey.

He scanned the front of the barn again. The suspect took off, sprinting across the clearing toward the woods. Blake jerked up his rifle. The man looked right at him, his eyes wide with panic. He lunged for the cover of some pine trees.

Pop, pop.

Missed. The man disappeared into the dark gloom of tree cover.

Blake cursed and straightened, knees popping from crouching so long, and took off in pursuit. When he reached where the man had entered the woods, he shook his head. The guy was about five foot five and probably weighed a buck thirty, if that. He should have been light on his feet, easily weaving his way through the thin early-spring vegetation without leaving much of a trace. Instead, he'd plowed through like a linebacker, heedless of breaking small branches and leaving clear footprints in the dew-laden grass. He might as well have put out a sign saying Bad Guy Went This Way. Either the guy was an idiot, or he was extremely clever, trying to lead Blake into an ambush.

Another birdcall chirped behind him, this one the not-so-convincing squawk of a blue jay. There was no mistaking SWAT team member Randy Carter's signal. Blake rolled his eyes. He doubted even a novice in the woods would think that was a real bird. He paused and glanced over his shoulder. Sure enough, Randy stood in the same copse that Blake had left just moments ago. Randy motioned for him to come back and made another motion toward his left.

Blake shook his head, held up one finger

and pointed down the path where the suspect had disappeared.

Randy insistently pointed to his left again.

Blake tightened his hand on his rifle in frustration. If Randy couldn't understand a simple signal, then that was his problem. Blake refused to put the team in danger by breaking off pursuit. The suspect could circle back around and sneak up on one of them, or he could escape altogether. Ignoring Randy, Blake headed into the woods.

Ten minutes later, he found the suspect. The man was holding his rifle above his head to keep it dry as he waded across a waist-deep stream.

Blake brought his rifle up and stepped from the cover of trees. "Police. Freeze."

The suspect whipped around.

Blake squeezed the trigger. *Pop.*

The suspect let out a blistering curse. A dark red stain covered his right shoulder. Blake took another shot, giving the man a matching stain on the left.

"I give up! Stop shooting!" The man held his gun over his head and glared at Blake.

Blake kept his rifle trained on him. "Work your way back to this side of the river. If you make any sudden movements, I'll pop you again."

The man's eyes narrowed with the promise of retribution, but he started forward as ordered.

After taking the man's gun, Blake pulled a set of handcuffs from the holder on the back of his belt.

The man's brows shot up. "Really? You're going to cuff me?"

"It's all part of the game, my friend. Turn around."

"You don't play fair. That second shot was completely unnecessary."

"I play to win. That's all that matters." He clicked the cuffs into place, slung the straps of both rifles over his shoulder and marched the man back toward the barn. Now that it was safe to break radio silence, he pulled the two-way off his belt and opened a channel.

"Blake to base. SWAT two, suspects zero. I got both of them. The first one in the barn, the second at the river. I'm on my way back with the second one."

His prisoner glanced over his shoulder, aiming a frown his way.

"Keep moving."

The man gave him a look that should have made him burst into flames.

The radio remained quiet as they strode toward the barn. No one answered Blake's call. He pressed the button again.

"Blake to base. Copy?"

No answer. Maybe they were in a communication dead zone. Cell phones were virtually useless out here. He supposed the same thing could happen even with their powerful radios. Or the equipment could be malfunctioning. Destiny was a small town with an equally small law-enforcement budget. Their equipment wasn't exactly top of the line and was rarely purchased new. The only reason that Destiny could even afford to have their detectives operate in a dual role as a SWAT team was that neighboring townships augmented the Destiny Police Department's budget. In return, Destiny SWAT responded to calls across several counties, when needed. But even the extra money never seemed to be enough.

When they moved into the clearing by the barn, Blake jerked to a halt and drew in a sharp breath. There, lying on the ground, were his teammates—everyone except their leader, Dillon. They were all dressed in green camouflage uniforms, covered with red splotches.

Chapter Two

Blake's prisoner started laughing. He was tempted to shoot the man again.

"I see you got your suspect," someone snarled close by.

He whirled around to see Dillon Gray striding toward him. Beside him, Chief Thornton's white puff of hair lifted and fell with every step he made. Both of them looked mad enough to wrestle hornets.

A sinking feeling settled in Blake's gut. What had he done wrong this time? He looked to his teammates for support. But they were all lying motionless on the ground. He cleared his throat and straightened his shoulders as Dillon stopped directly in front of him, the chief a few steps back.

"What happened?" Blake waved toward the team. "I don't understand. I took out the first suspect in the barn. I know he didn't get off any shots. And I followed this guy to the river."

"There were *three* suspects," Dillon snapped. "While you were off gallivanting alone, the third suspect ambushed the rest of the team."

Blake's gaze dropped to the red splotches on Dillon's chest that added weight to his accusation.

"But our intel said there were only two." Blake motioned toward his prisoner, who was still laughing, but was now sitting on top of a rotting log. "This guy took off, so I—"

Bam. White-hot pain exploded through Blake's jaw and he slammed back onto the ground. He glared up at Dillon, whose fist was still clenched as if he were ready to punch him again.

"What the hell was that for?" Blake snarled. "I got two of the bad guys."

"Yeah. You did. But you ignored the signals from both Randy and me and went all Rambo on your own." Dillon waved toward the bodies on the ground. "You weren't here when the team needed you."

Blake shoved to his feet. "I don't know what has you so fired up. If an entire team can't handle one bad guy without my help, you should be mad at them, not me."

"You idiot." Dillon took another step toward him.

The chief grabbed his shoulder. "Easy," Thornton said. Then he let Dillon's shoulder go and moved back, making it clear that he trusted his most senior officer to handle the situation. But he'd rather it not devolve into a fistfight.

Blake wanted to punch both of them. He'd done his job. It was the rest of the team who'd failed.

Dillon's jaw clenched and unclenched several times before he spoke again. "You can get up now," he told the team. "Everybody reload your paint guns and get fresh camo. We're doing this again until we get it right."

A chorus of grumbles sounded from the others as they stood. But they dutifully headed toward the stacks of supplies on the other side of the clearing, where their gear was laid out for the day's training exercises.

"Tim, you okay?" Dillon asked the man who'd played the suspect that Blake had "killed" in the river.

"A bit bruised. He shot me *twice*. That second one was out of pure meanness."

"Oh, for Pete's sake. You didn't go down," Blake said. "I had to make sure you were dead."

"I was in the water. What was I supposed to do? Go under?"

"It might have been more convincing."

The man swore.

Dillon waved Tim toward the other SWAT team members. "Have one of the others uncuff you. If you don't want to stay for round two, I understand. You'll get paid either way."

"Nah, that's fine. As long as *he* isn't part of the next exercise." He angled his chin toward Blake.

Blake rolled his eyes. The man was being melodramatic. But then Dillon stepped closer, blocking his view of their pretend-perpetrator.

"That won't be a problem," Dillon said. "Blake's not participating in any more training."

Blake frowned. "Why not?"

"Seeing your teammates lying dead on the ground isn't answer enough?"

He barely refrained from rolling his eyes. "You obviously staged that for effect."

"You're right. We did catch the third suspect. But it was a close thing. None of us knew there was a third one out here. The chief surprised us with that element, which just proves how important it is to always be alert and operate as a team, watching each other's backs." He poked Blake in the chest as if for emphasis. "You were supposed to watch your partner's back. But Donna said you took off without her halfway through the scenario. What was that about?"

Blake felt his face flush with heat. He glanced

toward the trucks. Donna had already changed into fresh camo and was retying her blond hair into a ponytail. She was also the only member of the team not paying attention to him and Dillon. Had he upset her? Did she feel that he'd let her down?

She'd been training him for several months, teaching him the Destiny Police Department's way of doing things, which wasn't the way he'd been trained in Knoxville. He was supposed to stick with her today. But when he'd seen the suspect racing through the woods, he'd taken off in pursuit, without waiting for his partner.

"I screwed up," he admitted. "I didn't want the suspect to get away, so I chased him to the barn. I assumed Donna would follow. But I lost her."

"No kidding. She was scanning the woods, searching for the suspects, and when she turned around, you were gone. Not exactly a team move."

Blake clenched his hands into fists at his sides. Not that he'd use them. He and Dillon were both a couple of inches over six feet and equally brawny. No doubt a fight between them would be long, bloody and painful. But that wasn't why Blake wouldn't hit him. Blake respected Dillon, even if the sentiment wasn't returned. He'd never raise his fists against him.

Too bad Dillon didn't share the same compulsion.

Blake waggled his jaw to ease the ache. "I had no reason to believe that Donna was in jeopardy. I would have come back to look for her, but the suspect holed up in the barn, giving me the perfect opportunity to pursue him. Once I took him out, the other suspect appeared. What was I supposed to do? Ignore him? Let him go?"

"What you're supposed to do, always, is follow orders. Your primary objective today was to stick with your partner. I made that crystal clear this morning. Failing that, when I signaled for you to report to me, you ignored my signal."

"I couldn't turn around. I would have missed my shot."

"You could have responded to me over the radio if you were worried about losing your sight line of the suspect. But you didn't."

"Not at first, no. I couldn't risk the noise alerting him. I did call later, after—"

"After the rest of the team was ambushed? And killed?"

Blake clamped his jaw shut. Why was he even trying to explain? As usual, Dillon refused to listen. He was a great leader and friend—to the *rest* of the team. But he'd disliked Blake from day one and made no secret about it. The only thing Blake could figure was that Dillon resented him because the chief had hired him without asking for his input.

If Chief Thornton hadn't offered him a job when he'd run into Blake at the Knoxville Police Station and gotten a taste of the drama going on there, Blake would be unemployed by now, with no prospects for another law-enforcement job. He owed a lot to the chief, including his silence about Blake's past. Blake hadn't wanted to share the details of what had happened, because he didn't want to prejudice his new team against him in case they didn't agree with his side of the story. But on days like today, he wondered if they'd both made a mistake. Their pact of silence meant that both of them had to lie to the team in answer to their questions about Blake's past. And lies were the worst sort of foundation on which to build trust. Which was why he always felt as though he were running in quicksand around here, never gaining traction no matter how hard he tried to fit in.

Except with Donna.

Beautiful and smart, she was the one bright spot in his life in Destiny, the one person who treated him as if he mattered. And he'd gone and screwed up with her, too. He'd run off after a suspect when he should have stuck by her side, training exercise or not. She probably despised him just as much as Dillon now.

He raised his hands in surrender, trying to defuse the situation. "Look, I'm sorry. I shouldn't have gone after the suspect on my own. I see that now."

"Gone off on your own? It's not that simple. You risked your partner's *life*. And don't you dare tell me it was *just* a paint-ball fight. This weekend's exercises are designed to test our instincts and improve our reactions, just as if this was the real thing. If this *was* the real thing, you just proved you can't be trusted to watch over your partner or follow instructions."

"You're overreacting. If this had been a true SWAT situation, I would have stayed with Donna."

Dillon shook his head. "You still don't get it. You can't act one way in training and plan on acting another way on an actual call. Training is supposed to make things second nature, so you'll react on muscle memory, without having to think about it. You have to treat every exercise like the real thing. Didn't they teach you that in the military?"

Blake stiffened and glanced at Thornton. But there was no help from that quarter. Thornton wouldn't even look him in the eye.

"Are we done here?" Blake demanded, his patience gone. There was only so much lecturing a grown man could take with his entire team a stone's throw away, witnessing his humiliation.

"Yeah. We're definitely done. Because you're toxic—always have been. You're a lone wolf, a rogue who has to do things his own way. People like you get people like me killed. The chief saw something in you when he hired you. I'll admit that I never did. But I worked with you, gave you every opportunity to prove my doubts wrong, to figure out how to be a member of this team. But all you've managed to do is prove me right. And I'm not willing to risk the lives of everyone here for your ego." He motioned toward Chief Thornton. "And neither is he. We both agree on this. It's over. Go home, Blake. You can turn in your equipment Monday morning. You won't need it anymore. You're fired."

Chapter Three

Donna entered the sleazy establishment that passed as a bar in this corner of Sevier County. Back in Destiny, this place would have been condemned and torn down, deemed unfit for even pigs to slop around in.

There was a plus side, though. It was quiet, too early in the evening to have more than a handful of patrons. And none of them had felt inclined to feed any money into the old-fashioned jukebox in the corner of the room.

Wrinkling her nose at the smell of urine and stale beer, she forced herself to step all the way inside, even though she was tempted to make an emergency run for a can of Lysol first.

A familiar figure sat on a bar stool at the far end, accepting what she hoped was his first drink of the night from the bartender. If Blake Sullivan was plastered, that was going to make her little crusade that much more difficult.

When he lifted the shot glass to his mouth, his hand shook and he sloshed some over the side. *So much for hoping that he wasn't plastered.* He downed the amber liquid in one swallow and wiped the back of his hand across his mouth. Donna flexed her hand against the pistol holstered at her waist. If it had been loaded with paint balls instead of nine-millimeter slugs, she'd have already shot him. She was that ticked.

"Hey, lady," the bartender called out. "No guns allowed in here."

Blake slowly looked at her, his reflexes obviously dulled by the liquor. A sober cop would have jerked around to assess the danger as soon as the bartender mentioned a gun.

She pulled her badge out of the pocket of her jeans and flashed it. "Cop."

The bartender's expression turned frosty, his eyes as dark and deadly looking as the ones on the cobra tattoo snaking up his neck. "Makes no difference to me. No guns."

"Don't worry. I'm not staying." She put her badge away and strode across the room, her boots echoing on the scarred hardwood floor. Stopping beside Blake's stool, she motioned toward the door. "Let's go."

He scowled at her. "Another whiskey." His words were slurred, his face ruddy.

The bartender stepped toward him with a

bottle of Jack Daniel's. Before he could refill the shot glass, Donna slapped her hand over it. "He's done."

"No. He's not." Blake yanked the glass away from her and held it out toward the bartender. "Fill 'er up."

The bartender lifted the bottle.

"He's drunk," Donna warned. "You pour that, and he gets behind the wheel, I'll arrest both of you."

He hesitated, shrugged and moved down the bar to a patron who promised to be less trouble.

Blake glared at her through bleary eyes. "This isn't Blount County. You can't arrest anyone here."

"He doesn't know that." She jerked her thumb toward the bartender.

Blake swiveled around and slouched back against the bar. "How did you find me?"

"Call tree."

He frowned. "Call what?"

She sighed. "One of many things you've failed to learn, even though I've told you about it before. Destiny's a very small town, so—"

He snorted. "No kidding."

She wanted to punch him. Instead, she forced a smile. "Unlike you, I consider Destiny's cozy size to be one of its many assets. Case in point, the call tree. Someone goes missing, I can make one call, and pretty soon, half the people in the county are looking out their windows. It's more efficient than a big city's AMBER Alert system."

His mouth quirked up. "You put out an AMBER Alert on me? I had no idea you cared so much."

"There are a lot of things you don't know," she grumbled. "Maybe you should pay more attention."

His brow crinkled in confusion, but his inebriated brain couldn't seem to grasp what she meant. Thank goodness. Admitting she cared about the brute while in a bar that smelled like pee wasn't something she wanted sober Blake to remember.

"My point is that one of the benefits of living in Destiny is that we watch out for each other. After a few calls, I knew you'd left town and what road you'd taken. Unfortunately, just like with my jurisdiction, my useful contacts end at the county line. So I had to do a bit of searching on my own after that."

He picked up his empty shot glass, frowned and thunked it back onto the bar. When he looked at her again, he blinked as if surprised that she was still there.

"What do you want?" he slurred.

She eyed the few people in the room, noting how closely they were paying attention to the exchange. It was bad enough that they were witness to Blake being drunk. If word got back to Chief Thornton or Dillon, there was no way she could fix what was probably already an unfixable situation and get them to rehire him.

"We need to talk. Alone."

He shook his head. "I'm not going anywhere. I like it here."

She snorted. "Yeah. It's real nice. Great ambience. You could mark your territory right where you're sitting, and I bet no one would bat an eyelash."

His brow wrinkled again. "Huh?"

She counted to ten and tried to remember all the reasons she liked this man enough not to shoot him with real bullets. But she couldn't seem to think of even one at the moment. "Just step outside so we can talk. You can drink yourself under the table later."

"Bar."

It was her time to frown in confusion. "What?"

"Drink myself under the bar." He thumped the polished surface for emphasis. "You called it a table."

"No, I..." She drew a deep breath. "Whatever. Let's go."

"Nope. You have something to say to me, say it right here. Then you can skedaddle on home and let me drink in peace." He waved toward the bartender and held out his glass.

The bartender took one look at Donna and shook his head. "Sorry, man. No can do."

She snatched the shot glass from him and set it out of his reach. When he opened his mouth to complain, she stepped closer, sandwiching her hips between his open thighs. The way his breath caught when she leaned in close would have been satisfying if she thought he was reacting to her as a woman. But as drunk as he was, there had to be another explanation. Like maybe the smell of shampoo and soap from her recent shower was too startling a contrast to the odor of urine and stale cigarettes he'd been basking in this afternoon.

She whispered in his ear. "You smell like a brewery, so I'm betting your bladder is full. I'm also betting you'd rather not wet yourself in front of all your lovely friends—which is exactly what you'll do if I have to come back in here with my Taser and take you on a five-second ride." She stepped back and shrugged. "Your choice. Walk out of here on your own with me. Or wait here for my Taser."

Her threat carried the weight of sincerity. She wasn't bluffing. He mumbled some coarse words and threw a few bills on the counter. But he didn't argue anymore as he stumbled after her to the parking lot outside.

When they reached her *previously* white Ford Escape, courtesy of the muddy back roads she'd slogged through to find him, she leaned against the front passenger door. A raindrop splatted on the top of her head.

She glanced up at the dark, ominous-looking clouds. The weatherman had predicted more thunderstorms tonight, which was why Dillon had cut their training exercise short. He'd wanted them to have enough time to thoroughly clean and stow their equipment, real guns or not, before it started to pour.

Normally Donna would have been right there with her teammates, helping out. But she'd been so upset over Blake getting fired that she couldn't focus and started making mistakes. Dillon had finally told her to go home and come back fresh in the morning for the second part of the training.

After a hot shower failed to make her feel any better, she'd done the only thing she could think to do. She'd called Blake. A lot. And texted. When that failed to get a response, she'd started to worry. That was when she'd put out a few feelers, trying to figure out where he might have gone.

Now, watching him sway on his feet in front of her, she was questioning her sanity in thinking she could undo the damage that he'd done today. After all, he'd accomplished what no one else had ever done.

He'd made Dillon Gray give up.

For goodness' sake, Dillon lived on a horse rescue ranch. He and his wife ran horse clinics every summer to help disabled and underprivileged children. He believed every living being could be helped or rehabilitated if given enough trust and support. For him to wash his hands of Blake was a shock that still had Donna reeling. But even if Dillon was ready to give up on him, she wasn't.

Not yet, anyway.

"I'll make this quick before we get soaked," she said. "I think Dillon overreacted. Calling you toxic, staging our fake deaths in that exercise to try to shock you and make his point, then firing you anyway, was a bit extreme."

"No kidding," he drawled, a note of bitterness creeping into his voice.

"But," she continued, "I do agree that you're not a team player. And he had every right to kick your butt after the stunts you pulled today."

Thunder sounded overhead. But it was nothing compared to the dark look in Blake's eyes as he stared down at her.

"I got two of the perpetrators all by myself. *Two*."

"Whoop-de-do. Any one of us could have done what you did. But that wasn't the point of the training."

He arched a brow. "Seriously? Catching the bad guys wasn't the point?"

"Well, yes, of course it was. But not on your own. The purpose was to teach us how to operate together, to have each other's backs."

"I need another drink." He started back toward the building.

She jumped in front of him, boots crunching on gravel as she shoved him against her car. "I drove halfway across this county looking for you. It was only through dumb luck that I drove past this place and saw your truck out front. The least you can do is listen to what I have to say."

He arched his brows. "Call tree didn't work the way you'd hoped, huh?" he mocked.

"You fool." She shoved him again. "I wouldn't have even known that you'd driven out this direction if it *hadn't* worked." Another raindrop plopped onto her cheek. She wiped it off and glared up at him.

"I never asked you to come after me," he said. "What the heck do you want, anyway?"

"What I want is to know that I didn't waste the last four months of my life trying to turn your sorry butt into a decent detective and SWAT team member. I've been showing you everything that I know—"

"Stuff I *already know*." He thumped his chest for emphasis. "This whole *teach me how to do things the Destiny way* is an insult. I was in the military before I became a cop. Surprisingly, I never once needed a babysitter. And I wasn't too shabby a detective in Knoxville after that. And yet you people all treat me like I'm a rookie. I've been putting away criminals just as long as any of you—longer than some. But you ignore any suggestions I make and criticize every little thing I do. You feel like you've wasted your time with me for the past four months? Welcome to my world, lady. I'm not exactly feeling like coming to Destiny was my smartest move either."

She blinked up at him, surprised at both his words and the hurt and resentment in his tone. Did he really feel that way? Or was it the liquor talking? He sure sounded coherent, even if his words were slurred. More important, could he be right? In their zeal to help him fit into the team, had they done just the opposite? Pushed him away?

"Blake, I don't know what to—"

He waved his hand in the air as if to erase their conversation and stepped to the side, forcing her to turn to face him.

"Forget it," he said, sounding angry and weary. "You wanna light me up with fifty-thousand volts? Be my guest. It won't be the first time I've been on that ride. But I'm not hanging around to listen to another lecture. I'm done." He started toward the bar.

"Blake, wait." When he didn't stop, she added, "Please."

He stiffened and halted in his tracks. But he didn't turn around.

She hurried over and stood in front of him. The defeated look on his face had guilt curling inside her even more. All along, she'd never once considered that the problem might be on both sides—maybe because blaming him was easier than facing her own failures.

"I'm sorry. Really, I am. I never meant to make you feel like you weren't a valued member of the team. It never occurred to me that—"

He shook his head. "Don't. Don't apologize, Donna. You've been the one good thing in my life since coming here. But it was a mistake coming here to begin with. *My* mistake. I was in a tough spot with…my career in Knoxville. And I took the easy way out, or thought I did, when the chief approached me about working for him. I should have known it was too good to be true."

She frowned. "A tough spot? The chief? Are you saying that he recruited you? I don't understand. Your file says you came here for a change in pace, to get away from the city grind. There wasn't any mention of the chief asking you to come here."

"My file." He laughed, sounding bitter again. "I wonder what else Thornton invented to cover for me."

"Blake, you're not making sense. What are you talking about? Were you in trouble? Why would he have to cover for you?"

He squeezed his eyes shut as if in pain and scrubbed his hands over the stubble on his jaw. "I'm drunk. Not making sense. Forget what I said." He dropped his hands to his sides. "Look, I appreciate you checking on me, making sure I was okay—assuming that's why you're here. But I'm a big boy. And it's time I started taking care of myself."

She stood in confusion, his little speech sparking all kinds of questions as he circled around the front of her car and headed toward his truck. All this time, she'd never once questioned his decision to leave his position on a large team in Knoxville to come here, probably because of her own bias in thinking that Destiny was the better choice. But to someone like Blake, who definitely didn't seem to care for small-town life, could the move have been considered a step down?

The pay had to be less, no question. But she'd figured the benefits of a smaller, more intimate team would have made up for it. To someone like her, it would. But now that she looked at it with fresh eyes, it really didn't make sense. Not for a guy who made no secret of his preference for cities over small towns. Then why had he come here? And what role had the chief played in his decision? More important, where would he go from here?

It wasn't until he wobbled and missed a step, nearly falling on top of the car next to his truck, that it dawned on her that she needed to intervene. She hurried after him, reaching his side just as he fit his key into the lock. Or tried to. He missed and scraped about six inches off the paint. She grimaced in sympathy. But before he could try again and do more damage, she swiped his keys.

"Hey, give those back." He grabbed for them, but she whirled around and ran for her car.

In spite of his wobbly gait, he caught her in

three strides. He grabbed her with one arm around her waist and whirled her around to face him. Good grief, he was strong. She pushed her hands against his chest but couldn't budge his viselike grip.

"Let me go."

"After you give me my keys." He held out his free hand, palm up.

She should have been angry. But she was still feeling guilty and confused over everything he'd said. And there was the distraction of how darn good his hard body felt against hers, and how wonderfully masculine he smelled. Even the whiskey on his breath didn't deter her ridiculous, unwanted response to being this close to him. Instead of pushing him away, she wanted to slide her hands up his chest and lock them behind his neck. Which was why she had to make him let her go. Now. Before she made a fool of herself.

She pinched his arm. Hard.

He snatched his arm back and rubbed where her nails had formed indentations on his skin. "What'd you do that for?"

"You're drunk."

"No kidding."

A drop of rain landed on her head. Then another. "Look, I just want to talk some sense into you. I came here to ask you to come back. You're a good cop, a solid detective. You—"

"Was," he interrupted. "I was a good cop. Past tense. Dillon fired me. Remember?" He squinted at her through the smattering of raindrops that were starting to fall faster.

"Maybe we can fix that. Dillon has scheduled another training exercise at nine tomorrow morning. If you show up in your gear, like you're ready to try again, you can talk to him, apologize—"

"Apologize? You're kidding, right? He said I was *toxic*. You think an apology is going to change his opinion?"

"I think it would be a great start."

He shook his head. "There's no point in talking to Dillon. His mind is made up."

"So, that's it?" she said. "You're just going to quit?"

"I...was...fired." He enunciated each word slowly and concisely, as if she were hard of hearing. "I don't have a choice. My career in Destiny is over. Finished. There's nothing I can do." He held his hand out again. "We're about to get soaked. Give me my keys, and I'm out of your life forever."

His words took the breath right out of her. Did he really not care about her at all? What was she to him? Not even a friend whom he would miss? More angry than concerned about his welfare at this point, she whirled around and dashed toward her car.

This time, the element of surprise was on her side. Or maybe the rain slowed him down. She'd just gotten her driver's door closed and locked when he reached her. His shoes slid across the gravel as he tried to stop. But he ended up slamming against her door and grabbing her side mirror to keep from falling on his face.

He swore and straightened. Then he yanked her door handle a few times before leaning down to glare at her through the window. The clouds chose that moment to open up. Rain pelted down on him in sheets, drenching him in seconds. He hunched his shoulders against the onslaught, his dark eyes promising retribution through the glass.

"I need my keys," he yelled to be heard over the thunder and rain. He rapped his knuckles on the window. "Keys."

"You're drunk," she yelled back. "You have no business driving. Walk home." She dropped his keys onto the seat beside her and started the engine.

He slammed his hand against the roof of her car, making her jump. "My house is over twenty miles away."

"I can give you a ride home. But your truck stays here."

"No."

They glared at each other through the window. Him probably hating her. Her hating herself for having wasted so much time on him, both personally and professionally. Maybe she should give up on men entirely. They weren't worth the trouble.

She put her foot on the brake and shifted into drive.

His eyes narrowed. "Donna, don't you dare—"

She slammed the accelerator and zoomed out of the parking lot.

Chapter Four

Where was Blake, and was he okay? Those two questions had been worrying Donna all evening, ever since she'd left him standing in the rain, yelling after her.

She sat in her recliner, her legs tucked underneath her, while she cradled a cup of hot chocolate in her hands. It wasn't that the house was cold. Outside, it was only mildly chilly, and then only when the winds blew down from the nearby mountains. But she didn't need cold weather as an excuse to have hot chocolate. It was her poison of choice when she needed soothing.

Tonight, she definitely needed soothing.

Across the room, the TV screen hung over the fireplace, dark and quiet. Typically, unless her mom or one of her mom's well-meaning klatch of friends had set her up on yet another disastrous blind date, she would spend Saturday nights binge-watching recorded cop shows.

The ones with the fake forensics and technology were the most entertaining. Where an investigator could search a single database and come up with a person's entire life history in seconds—like what books that person had checked out of the library in kindergarten and never returned. Nothing could make her laugh harder than their implausible, ridiculous storylines. But tonight, instead, she stared at the set of keys on the coffee table. Blake's keys.

And she wasn't laughing.

Guilt was riding her hard. Not for taking his keys. She'd probably saved his life, or someone else's, by not letting him drive. But she shouldn't have left him in that parking lot with no way home. She should have argued with him until he agreed to get in her car. She could have taken him back later—once he was sober—to get his truck.

Where was he now? What was he doing? She had absolutely no clue. When she left him, she'd driven away for all of fifteen minutes before guilt had sent her back to that rancid-smelling bar. But even though his black pickup was still sitting in the gravel right where she'd left it, Blake wasn't.

The bartender had only shrugged when she asked him where Blake had gone. She suspected he knew the answer. But he had no inclination to tell her. Four hours later, with the clock edging close to midnight, Blake still hadn't responded to any of her calls or texts.

Not that she could blame him.

If he'd left her in that parking lot, she'd be furious. For days. Maybe longer. Mama always said her temper ran hotter than a busted radiator and cooled just as slowly.

She let out a heavy sigh and set her still-full cup on the side table. There was no use delaying the inevitable any longer. No amount of chocolate or silly cop shows were going to make her relax. And there was no point in trying to sleep. How could she even try to close her eyes when he could be lying hurt somewhere, maybe passed out in a ditch?

That lovely image had crossed her mind so many times that she'd called the emergency room in Maryville to see if he'd been brought in. The state police and the dispatch operators for both Blount and Sevier Counties had no reports on him either. She should have been relieved. Instead, she was more worried than ever. It was as if he'd vanished.

Okay—that was it. She absolutely couldn't sit here any longer, waiting for a call that was never going to come. She would have to head back out and find him herself. Again. And this time, she wasn't leaving until he was safe and sound at home.

After retrieving her holster and pistol from the floor beside her chair, she went into her bedroom to change out of her nightshirt. A few minutes later, dressed in jeans and a simple button-up blouse, she headed toward the front door.

A loud knock had her whipping out her pistol and flattening herself against the wall beside the door. Her pulse rushed in her ears. Who would be pounding on her door this late? Or even at all? Saying that she lived in the boonies was an understatement. Visitors willing to drive out this far from town, this far from *anything*, were extremely rare. Even her own family was loath to make the trip and bounce down the pothole-filled street in front of her house. Donna was the one who usually made the long trek to see them instead.

The knock sounded again. "Donna?" Blake's deep voice bellowed. "I know you're up. I saw you through the front window."

Blake. He was okay. *Thank God*. Her shoulders dropped, the tension draining out of her as she holstered her gun and reached for the dead bolt. Then his words sank in. She hesitated, without opening the door. "Why were you peeping in my window?"

"I wasn't *peeping*."

She could practically hear him roll his eyes.

"Your lights are on, and the blinds are open," he continued. "I could see you from halfway down that death trap out front that you call a road. The suspension on my truck is probably shot now. What'd you do? Tick the mayor off, and now he won't send the city out to maintain your street?"

She flipped the dead bolt and pulled open the door. "Actually, it's his wife. She sped through a school zone, so I radioed for a patrol unit and followed her to city hall. She didn't appreciate me detaining her until the uniformed officer got there. And she especially didn't like the two-hundred-fifty-dollar ticket."

His brows rose as he stepped inside. "Did you know who she was when you saw her speeding?"

"Yep. Honestly, I probably wouldn't have bothered if she'd blown by me out on the highway. It's not like we have enough traffic around here to worry about her causing an accident. But she could have run someone's kid over. That's an unforgivable sin in my book. So if the price of making her stop and think next time is a bumpy ride home every day, I'll pay it." She winced. "But I do need to get a four-wheel drive if this vendetta goes on much longer. My little SUV isn't designed for that kind of punishment.

It's already starting to rattle, and it's only a few years old."

He smiled. "I didn't know you had a soft spot for kids. Why haven't I heard this story before?"

She cocked her head. "Why haven't you ever visited my house before? And why haven't you invited me to yours? We're partners. We should kick back together after work sometimes, or on weekends."

His smile faded. "The answer to those questions are irrelevant, since I'm not a cop anymore."

She shook her head. "Once a cop, always a cop. And as far as I'm concerned, this current situation with Dillon is temporary."

"That's actually why I'm here. Partly, anyway." He waved toward the two leather couches and recliner a few feet away. "Mind if we talk for a few minutes? Or is the open door an unsubtle social signal that I should leave?"

She blinked, surprised to realize that she was still holding on to the doorknob. "Sorry. Go on, have a seat." She shut the door behind him and followed him into the part of the house that functioned as a family room.

He perched on the edge of one of the two couches, resting his forearms on his thighs with his hands clasped together. She didn't think she'd ever seen him look so unsure of himself.

His confidence in everything that he did was one of the things that had always bugged Dillon, because he took it as arrogance. He expected the new guy to show more humility and work harder to fit in. Until Blake's little speech in the parking lot earlier, she'd thought pretty much the same thing. Now she wasn't sure what she thought.

"Nice place," he said as she sat beside him on the couch. "It looks a lot bigger inside than it does from the outside."

"It's the vaulted ceiling and the open concept. My dad helped me with the remodel. Took a couple of years. That was a long time ago, though. It's about ready for another update— new lights, new plumbing fixtures. The floors could use refinishing. But I don't have the free time I used to, before I added part-time SWAT officer to my full-time detective duties."

"You and your dad did all the work?"

"Most of it. We rooked my three sisters' husbands into helping with the heavy lifting. But for the most part, it was me and Dad. With Mom supervising, of course. She's a worse back seat renovator than any back seat driver." She waved toward the kitchen, which was separated from the rest of the room by a butcher block island. "You want a beer or something?"

His brows arched again. "I think we both

know I had more than my quota of alcohol earlier today. But thanks."

"Right." She rubbed her hands on her jeans, hating the awkwardness that had settled between them. "I see you have your—"

"I wanted to ask you—"

They both stopped and smiled.

He waved at her. "You first."

She cleared her throat. "I was just going to ask how you got here. Since I, um, have your keys."

"My neighbor. I called him and he was just a few miles away, running an errand. We both have spare sets of each other's keys in case we lock ourselves out of our homes or cars. He and his son picked me up at the bar. His son drove my truck home while I slept off the liquor. In case you were wondering how I got my truck back."

"I tried to call—"

He pulled his phone out of his pocket and tapped the glass before turning it around. "I noticed."

The home screen showed fifteen missed calls.

Her face flamed hot. "Are all of those from me?"

"Every one."

"Wow. I didn't realize I'd been that big a pest."

"You texted even more than you called." He

smiled and put the phone away. "I came over here for a couple of reasons. The first was to apologize."

She frowned. "What would you apologize for? I'm the one who left you stranded, in the rain, at a horrible, smelly bar. In my defense, I did eventually turn around and go back. But you were gone."

"Yeah, this is the part where I have to admit that I hid in the men's room when you came back into the bar looking for me. Not one of my prouder moments. But I was still angry and didn't want to talk to you."

"I *knew* that snake-tattooed bartender was lying. Well, at least you're okay. And you didn't end up with your truck in a ditch somewhere."

His jaw tightened. "Believe it or not, I'm not the bad guy everyone seems to think I am. And unlike the mayor's wife, I care about the other people out on the road. I would never drink and drive, in spite of how I acted earlier. The fact that you thought I would only contributed to my foul mood, so I didn't bother to tell you that all I was going to do was lie down in my truck and sleep it off."

"Blake, I didn't mean that the way it—"

He held up his hand again. "Please, let me get all this out before you think I'm blaming you for my own actions. I'm not. I was a jerk to you today. You were worried about me." He patted his pocket where he'd put his cell phone. "Obviously. And I didn't have the decency to answer even one of your calls or texts to let you know that I was okay. I'm really sorry, Donna. And even though I'd argue it wasn't necessary to take my keys, and it wasn't fun being left standing in the rain, it *was* a wake-up call. The whole day was a wake-up call, in a lot of ways. I hope you can accept my deepest, heartfelt apology. Can you forgive me?"

He startled her by taking one of her hands between his, while he watched her and waited for her reply. She swallowed hard, trying to remember what he'd even said. It was hard to focus when his large, warm hands held hers and he was staring at her with such intensity.

The man had definitely missed his calling. Instead of law enforcement, he should have been a sexy leading man in Hollywood, making all the women swoon and throw themselves at his feet. All it would take was one look from those intense, dark blue eyes to make the rest of the world fade away. She didn't think he'd ever looked at her this way before. It was doing funny things to her belly, and her pulse was racing so fast, it was a wonder he didn't say something about it.

He'd showered recently. His short, nearly

black hair was still damp. And he was wearing fresh clothes—jeans, boots and a blue pullover shirt that made his eyes look an even darker blue than usual.

Not that any of that mattered.

She shouldn't care how gorgeous he looked, or how incredibly wonderful his warm skin felt against hers. But he'd never focused the full force of his attention on her before, not like this, as if the only thing that mattered in the world was her.

"Donna? Help me out here. I have no idea what that sharp mind of yours is thinking right now. Are you about to forgive me, or should I run for my truck before you pull out your gun?" His mouth quirked up in a half grin that had her toes curling against the floor.

Good grief, what was wrong with her? She was obviously more tired than she'd thought. And the day's events had made her emotions raw. Blake the police officer she could handle. Blake the sexy, nice, attentive man sitting across from her—holding her hand—was draining her IQ points by the second. If she didn't do something fast, she'd start stuttering and batting her eyelashes at him. Or worse, lunge across the couch and find out once and for all if he was the excellent kisser that she'd always fantasized that he would be.

His brows crinkled with concern. "Donna? Are you okay? You look flushed." He reached toward her face as if to check her for a fever.

She jerked back and yanked her hand free. Popping up from the couch, she said the first thing that flashed into her mind. "I have to pee."

His eyes widened.

She groaned and sprinted from the room.

WHAT HAD JUST HAPPENED? Blake stared at the empty spot on the couch beside him where Donna had been sitting just seconds earlier. Obviously he'd upset her, or she wouldn't have run out of the room like that. But other than an apology, he couldn't figure out how he'd managed to make things worse.

He blew out a frustrated breath and stood. He was too agitated to keep sitting on the couch, so he paced back and forth in front of the fireplace. Now that he'd delivered his pathetic apology, with disastrous results, he wasn't even sure whether he should hang around to tell her the other reason that he was here. After all, there were dozens of explanations for his concerns— all of which seemed valid and far more likely than the insane scenario that kept running through his head. Maybe he should have started with the scenario and skipped the apology part.

But he'd been worried that she'd be too angry to listen if he didn't smooth things over first.

A lot of good that had done.

He checked his watch. Thirty minutes to midnight on a Saturday. This was silly. He should just go home and try to sleep off the aftereffects of a very nasty hangover that was already making his head pound in spite of the aspirin he'd taken. Everything was bound to look different in the morning. His concerns would be proven false, and everyone would go about their lives like normal.

Except for him.

Nothing had been normal in his life for a very long time.

"Blake."

He turned to see Donna standing by the recliner, her brow lined with worry. He cleared his throat and stepped over to her. "Whatever I did, if my apology somehow offended you, I'm truly sorry. I didn't mean to—"

"What? No, no. You did nothing wrong. It was just…" She shook her head. "Forget it. It was something stupid. Nothing to worry about. I'm just glad you're okay."

"Then we're good? You're not upset with me?"

"I'm upset that you got yourself fired. And I'll be really upset if you don't try to talk to Dillon to get your job back. Maybe if you just apologize to him, explain your side—"

"That's why I'm here. I mean, other than trying to fix things between you and me. I came here because I did try to contact Dillon. I wanted to meet with him, just the two of us, and talk this thing out."

"Oh, well, that's great. We're supposed to go back to Hawkins Ridge for another exercise in the morning, around nine. Maybe you could go up there and talk to him then, while the rest of us are getting everything set up." She frowned. "Why are you giving me a funny look? What's wrong?"

"It could be nothing."

"Tell me."

Lightning flashed off in the distance, illuminating the front windows. A distant boom of thunder followed. And still, he couldn't seem to force the words out. The longer he stood there, the more he felt like he'd jumped the gun. The whiskey and his hangover were dulling his brain, not to mention the lateness of the hour.

"Well?" she prompted.

"Forget it. It's stupid. I'll do what you said, try to catch Dillon in the morning before your training session. Sorry I bothered you so late." He circled around her and headed for the door. He'd just flipped the dead bolt and was reaching for the doorknob when she grabbed it instead. He looked at her in question.

"You're not leaving yet. Something bothered you enough to come over here close to midnight to talk to me. It wasn't just to tell me you were sorry. What's going on? Talk to me."

He dropped his hand and shook his head. "Forget it. I'm sure it's just the storm interfering with signals. Or maybe they're all too ticked at me to answer. I ignored dozens of texts and calls from you, and it didn't mean I needed help."

"Blake, if you don't start making sense, I swear I'm going to shoot you."

By the irritated look on her face, he didn't doubt that she would. He let out a deep breath and prepared himself for her laughter. "Dillon's missing."

She blinked. Then blinked again.

"See?" he said. "Told you it was stupid. It's nonsense. I went off half-cocked and still half-drunk and imagined all sorts of crazy things. I'm sure he's fine." He reached for the doorknob, motioning for her to move her hand.

She suddenly stood on her tiptoes, leaned in close and sniffed.

He jerked back. "What are you doing?"

"Seeing if I can smell whiskey on your breath."

He gritted his teeth. "I'm not drunk. I haven't touched a drop since you left me at the bar."

"And yet you said that Dillon's missing. What does that mean?"

The smile hovering on her lips had him feeling even more ridiculous. "I wanted to talk to him, like I said. So as soon as I sobered up, I called, both cell phone and radio. He didn't answer."

She shrugged. "Why would he? He fired you. I doubt he ever wants to talk to you again. Which is why you need to go see him in person—"

"I did. I went to his horse ranch. He wasn't there. Neither was his wife and daughter. The guy who oversees the operations—"

"Griffin."

He nodded. "Griffin. He said Mrs. Gray and her daughter had gone off on some cruise. But he didn't know where Dillon was. He figured he was still in the woods, conducting training exercises."

"What time was this?"

"Close to nine, I imagine."

She glanced past him, probably to the wall clock that he'd noticed over the TV earlier. "It's way too late to try calling him again. I'm sure he's okay, though. Dillon's one of the most capable men I know. He—"

"I called Randy, too."

"Okay. What did he say about Dillon?"

"Nothing. Randy didn't answer his phone either."

Her brow furrowed. "That's not like him. Even if he was upset, which is a rare thing for him, he wouldn't have ignored your call."

"That was my thought, too. So I called Max. Then Chris. I even tried the chief, on his home phone. No one answered any of my calls. I would have at least expected the chief's wife to answer."

She shook her head. "She's on the cruise with Ashley. All the team's wives went—Dillon's wife, Ashley, and their baby, the chief's wife, Claire, Max's wife, Bex, and Chris's wife, Julie. It's a law-enforcement family cruise some charity put together, a getaway for the families who do so much to support their law-enforcement loved ones. That's how it was advertised, anyway. That's why Dillon scheduled the training this weekend. I could have sworn you knew all this. Scenic Cruises? Out of Miami? It was organized by some charity group out of Knoxville. I'm sure Dillon mentioned it."

"I'm sure he mentions lots of things to you. He and I rarely speak unless he's ordering me around or telling me I screwed up." He waved his hand in the air. "Forget it. That's not the point. I tried calling all of them tonight. No one answered. It's highly likely that they're ignoring me because of what happened today, and I overreacted. But I couldn't ignore it without letting you know. Just in case."

"Just in case what?"

He fisted his hands at his sides, feeling like an idiot. But he'd gone this far. He might as well go all in. "In case the entire SWAT team was abducted. Minus you and me, of course."

She blinked again. Then she started laughing.

He endured her laughter for a full minute. He couldn't take more than that. He brushed her hand off the doorknob and yanked open the door.

"Blake, wait. I'm sorry. Please don't go. I shouldn't have laughed at you. But you know cell service around here is awful. Your calls probably didn't even go through."

Since her voice was still laced with laughter, he didn't bother to reply. He strode out of the house and took the porch steps two at a time.

"Blake?"

He hopped into his truck and took off down the road, punching the gas to give free rein to his sour mood and temper. That was when he hit the first huge pothole. The front right tire slammed into the hole, and the entire truck lurched at a sickening angle before the tire popped out again. He cursed and was forced to slow to a near crawl. It took him a good ten minutes just to reach the end of the street-from-hell.

A flash of white zoomed at him from the left. He jerked around to see Donna's white Ford Escape barreling onto the road from an overgrown field. He swore and slammed his brakes, skidding and coming to a bouncing halt just a few feet from her driver's side door.

She stopped too, her face looking pale and drawn as she stared at him through her driver's side window, illuminated by his headlights. Before he could even unbuckle his seat belt, she was out of her SUV and running to his passenger door. He pushed the button to roll down the window.

"What the hell was that for?" he demanded. "You almost made me run right into you."

"I called them," she said. "The whole team. No one answered. I sent a group text. Nothing." She swallowed, looking visibly shaken. "I even tried the radio. All I got was static. It's not raining anymore. We can't blame the storm now. I can see them not answering your calls. But they wouldn't worry me like this. My God, Blake. What's going on?"

He popped open the passenger door. "Get in."

Chapter Five

Blake slowed his truck to turn down a gravel road that would lead them to the wooded area where they'd conducted the paintball exercise that morning. Beside him, Donna clutched a flashlight in her hands, anxiously staring through the windshield.

"What happened after I left Hawkins Ridge?" he asked. "Did Dillon take the team to another training site, maybe in one of those communication dead zones? Since you didn't have a partner at that point, I would guess he sent you home early. Maybe they decided to stay late, or came back for round two long after you were gone." He steered around a rut in the road.

"No. I mean, yes. Both." She swiped at her bangs, something she rarely did unless she was upset. "After Dillon…ordered you to leave, I…uh…went home early. Like you said. You know, because I didn't have a partner."

"Okay. He continued the training without you,

then. Like I said, the communications might not be working. Or maybe the storm caught them by surprise, and they had to wait it out. A rain-swollen creek could have prevented them crossing, and they're sitting it out until it goes down."

"No. That's not it. He *did* send me home early. But training was over for the day. All that was left was for the team to clean the equipment and stow it in their trunks for next time. You know what a stickler Dillon is about maintaining equipment, even fake guns. Cleaning them and prepping the gear for the trip back would have taken a good half hour, maybe forty-five minutes. But he wouldn't have kept anyone longer than that. He kept up with the weather reports, knew a storm was moving in. No way would he risk anyone's safety by having them out in the middle of it. I'm telling you, they're not training."

The gravel ended, and the remaining fifty yards of road was dirt. The truck bounced around the last curve, and the clearing was revealed up ahead. But it wasn't empty. Five trucks sat parked side by side, exactly as they'd been that morning. Blake gave Donna a puzzled glance as he parked beside them. He killed the engine and looked over at the obviously empty vehicles.

"Why would they still be up here?" he asked.

"It doesn't look like the vehicles have moved at all. I thought you said Dillon wanted everyone home, safe, with the storm coming in."

"He did." Her voice was quiet and strained, her face pale with worry for her friends. She opened her door.

"Wait. Did you call the station when you were making all those calls earlier?"

"Yes. The chief and the team hadn't checked in. But I was careful not to alarm the skeleton night staff. I was blasé in how I asked the question."

"Fair enough," he said. "Let's see if there's a reasonable explanation, or whether we need to raise the alarm after all."

He left the engine running with the headlights on to help them see better. But even with that, and a bright moon overhead, it was difficult to see much beyond the beams of their flashlights.

They took turns shouting out to the team. But no one answered. After a few minutes of searching, they were back at the parking area, with no clue about where their friends had gone.

Or, rather, where Donna's friends had gone.

To Blake, they'd always been just coworkers. Now, after he'd been fired, they weren't even that. But they all bled blue. If something had happened, he was darn well going to do everything he could to help them.

Whether they wanted him to or not.

"Maybe there was a medical emergency," Blake theorized. "If they stayed up here awhile after you left—maybe to do another training exercise—and they got caught in the storm—"

"Dillon wouldn't let that happen. He would have gotten them out of here before the storm let loose."

Her steadfast trust in Dillon was a little irritating. Blake didn't think the man could walk on water the way Donna did. "He's not a meteorologist. Let's assume for a moment that he misjudged the storm, that after you left he decided they should train a little longer, and they got caught out here. They took shelter somewhere, maybe in the old barn, where our fake perpetrator was hiding during the paint ball exercise. They could have holed up inside to wait out the storm. After the lightning stopped, something else happened. Maybe the chief had a heart attack, or one of them got cut or something. So they needed to take him back down the mountain to get him help."

He pointed to the puddles still in the dirt, the wet spots on the trunks of the trees closest to the clearing. "Judging by the way the slope runs here, this parking lot is probably like a bowl in the rain. It could have been a small lake by the time the storm passed, and they couldn't get to their vehicles."

"So they just, what, trekked through the woods and got lost? Even if someone was hurt and they had to hoof it down the mountain, where are they now? They grew up around here. Getting lost isn't something that would happen."

"What else could have happened? I don't see any tire tracks or footprints. No signs of anyone else coming up here. In spite of my fears earlier, foul play against an entire SWAT team seems hard to believe."

"A SWAT team with fake guns," she said, her voice quiet. "Dillon was all about safety. He made us lock up our real guns and ammo while we did the exercises. He didn't want to risk an accidental shooting."

He studied her. "What are you saying? That instead of accepting that they could be lost in the woods, you think someone came up here and...what? What did he do with them?"

"No, I'm not saying that at all. I'm just throwing out the facts as we know them. The team drove up but didn't drive back down. They aren't answering their phones, radios or us yelling at the top of our lungs. Something bad must have happened."

Her voice was barely above a whisper the next time she spoke. "I think we may be in over our heads. We should call the station, get some volunteers out here to help us conduct a more thorough search. Even if they're not lost, they could be stranded somewhere, maybe in a cell phone and radio dead zone. Obviously something happened to them or their vehicles wouldn't still be here."

"Agreed. We need to get some help out here."

He raised his flashlight beam, training it straight ahead, slicing a path of light through the darkness of trees and bushes about twenty feet away. "While you make that call, I'm going to go deeper in to check that barn and the clearing in front of it. There have to be some footprints there, maybe a piece of torn fabric caught on a branch. I'd like to find some tangible proof that might show us where the team was last. The trackers will want to start from the last known position."

She shoved her cell phone back into her pocket. "We're not splitting up. I'm your partner. We'll check it out together. *Then* I'll call this in."

The wobble in her voice had him hesitating. He looked down at her, noted the intensity in her expression, the shine of unshed tears sparkling in her eyes. He'd been with Destiny P.D. since late fall of the previous year and had been her partner for over four months. In all that time, she'd always been decisive, in control, never breaking down no matter how tough things got. He'd never once seen her rattled. But right now she seemed…fragile, vulnerable. And he'd bet it wasn't just because she was worried about her friends. There was something else going on here. And he thought he knew what it was.

"Donna?"

"Yeah?"

"It's not your fault."

She frowned. "What's not my fault?"

"Whatever happened, whatever is going on with the team. I think you're second-guessing yourself, feeling guilty. But if anyone's to blame, it's me. If I'd been a good partner to you, we'd have both been here with them when—"

"When what? When aliens beamed them up to the mother ship? Come on, Blake. This is crazy. Four highly trained SWAT team members and the chief of police don't just disappear off the face of the earth. You know what I'm starting to think is going on? Group hysteria, or mass hysteria, or whatever psychologists call it. We're both feeding off each other's fears and making this into something it's not."

"I honestly hope you're right."

"But you don't think I am."

"I didn't say that." Before she could interrogate him about what he really thought, he said,

"How about we finish our due diligence and get this over with? This whole place is giving me the creeps."

"You won't get any argument from me about that," she mumbled, scanning left and right with her flashlight, before training it in front of her again.

They headed into the woods, side by side. The truck's headlights didn't penetrate more than a dozen feet in, because trees blocked the light. Forced to rely solely on their flashlights and the moonlight overhead, they studied the ground, the branches and the bark of trees they passed.

When they stopped by a tree with red and blue paint splotches on it, Donna gave a small smile. "So much for Dillon's claim that our biodegradable paint will fade in the first rain. He's not going to be happy about that. He'll probably drop the vendor and start researching a new one." Her smile died a quick death as fears for her friends obviously invaded her thoughts. She stalked past the tree, and he rushed to catch up.

"Why didn't you tell me about the law-enforcement family cruise?" he asked, trying to steer her thoughts to more innocuous ones while they performed their search.

She hesitated, then continued forward, sweeping her flashlight across the ground. "Honestly, I guess it never occurred to me to bring it up in conversation. It's not like you ever social-ize with the rest of us after work. Not very often, anyway. I'm not even sure you've ever met Chris's wife, Julie. And you probably only know Max's wife, Bex, from your first real case with us last year, when someone was trying to kill her. Dillon's wife, Ashley, of course, every-one knows. The station would probably riot if she ever stopped dropping off her homemade treats."

"She does bake a mean oatmeal raisin cookie."

"Banana nut bread. That's my favorite. Her recipe is to die for, and she refuses to share it. Trust me, I've asked. Many times. That stuff is amazing." She pressed a hand to her heart as if paying homage.

"Yuck on bananas," he said. "Not my thing."

"No banana pudding?"

He wrinkled his nose. "Not even if I was starving."

"No wonder you don't fit in with the team," she teased. "Banana pudding is a staple of any well-balanced diet. Especially in the South."

"And yet somehow I've survived all these years without it." He stopped and looked around. "This is about where I first spotted the guy I ended up shooting in the second floor of the barn."

"Larry. The second guy, the one you caught

at the river, was Tim. Mike was the third guy. I don't think you ever saw him though."

He supposed he should have known the first two men's names. Maybe she and Dillon were right, and he really wasn't making enough of an effort to fit in. He'd really never accepted the blame for how things were going, always thinking it was everyone else's fault that they refused to accept an outsider. The truth, as with most things, was probably somewhere in the middle.

"Were Larry, Tim and Mike with the team when you left?"

She put her hand on his arm, her eyes widening as she pulled him to a stop. "Mike had to leave early. But Larry and Tim were still there. I didn't even think about calling them. If one of them answers, maybe they know where the guys went. Or, heck, maybe for some reason, they all piled into Tim and Larry's trucks and went to a bar somewhere, and it's too loud to hear their phones. With the wives out of town, it makes sense. They're having a guys' night out. Why didn't I think about that? Maybe Tim and Larry are the designated drivers. I bet we're going to feel really silly in about one minute. I just know it."

"I'm all for silly. It beats the alternative."

She checked her watch and winced. "If they're not in a bar, if they're back at Larry or

Tim's house, sleeping off a binge, someone's not going to be happy about being woken up at one in the morning. But no way am I waiting until a decent hour to call. Which unlucky soul gets woken up? Larry or Tim?"

"I think Tim suffered enough being shot twice. I vote for Larry."

"Larry it is." After tucking her flashlight under her arm, she scrolled through her contact list and punched the send button.

A few seconds later, she crossed her fingers in the air and spoke into the phone. "Larry? Yeah, hi. This is Detective Waters. Donna, that's right. Hey, I'm really sorry to call so late, but it's important. What? Oh, yes. I'm fine. Sorry. You?"

She made an impatient rolling motion with her hand as she waited for Larry to finish whatever he was babbling about.

Blake didn't wait. If it was taking this long to get anything out of Larry, and she had to call Tim, too, he could at least check the barn out, since it was visible through a gap in the trees up ahead. He motioned toward the gap, and she gave him a helpless gesture, pointing at the phone. He smiled and headed toward the barn, sweeping his flashlight back and forth.

The dilapidated structure was just as he remembered it—a sagging collection of warped gray boards, which were partially covered in vines that should have given up the ghost a long time ago. He figured it was similar to many other old structures throughout the Smokies, like those found near Cades Cove. It was a relic of another century. But unlike its cousins that were protected because they were in the Smoky Mountains National Park, this one was clearly suffering from a lack of historical society preservation.

If the building could talk, he imagined it would have some amazing stories to tell, the same way old men liked to rock on front porches, reliving the glory days with anyone who would listen. He smiled at that thought and pulled one of the large double doors open.

And froze.

Footsteps sounded behind him.

"Blake? Larry wasn't out in a bar with them. And Tim—"

He whirled around to stop her, but it was too late. She'd already seen inside. Her eyes widened with horror at what was visible in the beam of her flashlight.

"Oh, no. No, no, no. Oh, please, God. *No.*"

She dropped to her knees beside the bullet-riddled body of SWAT officer and fellow detective Randy Carter.

Chapter Six

Donna tried to peel Blake's hands off her arms. He was crouched beside her and wouldn't let her touch Randy.

"Let me go," she pleaded. "I have to check for a pulse. Maybe we can still save him."

"It's way too late for that. The blood's already starting to dry. He's gone." He gave her a light shake. "Donna, look in my eyes, not at him. Trust me, you don't want this to be the last image of your friend burned into your brain. You don't want to remember him this way for the rest of your life."

She was still trying to pry his fingers off her, but the anguish in his voice cut through her own haze of grief and despair and made her pause. Part of her had known that Randy was beyond help. But part of her was in denial, or had been. Blake's tone had snapped that second part back to reality.

She shifted her gaze to his. The hollowness

and pain in his dark eyes nearly stole her breath. What was he remembering from his own past? What kind of tragedy would put those shadows in someone's eyes? Without even thinking about it, she cupped his cheek.

He ducked away, forcing her to drop her hand.

"Come on," he said, his voice gentle but strained, all signs of whatever he'd been thinking about erased from his expression. "Let's make that call to the station."

"But—"

"But nothing. Randy was your friend. You shouldn't be here, cop or not. The best way to help him now is to leave the crime scene to others to process."

He didn't give her a chance to argue. He scooped her up in his arms and carried her out of the barn. She was so surprised that she didn't think to protest until he was lowering her back to standing.

She smoothed her shirt down and straightened her shoulders. "I'm a police officer first, a woman second. And I've spent half of my life working hard to ensure that I'm treated with the same respect that my male peers are treated. So don't you dare ever try to carry me like that again unless we're lovers and you're carrying me to bed. Got it?"

His eyes widened, and she could feel her face

flaming over her poor choice of words. But in that one moment, with him carrying her from a crime scene, all her struggles, the fights to be treated with respect in a profession dominated by men, came boiling to the surface. She would grieve, bitterly, for her longtime friend later. But right now she needed to be the best cop—the best detective—she could be so they could catch the killer and find the rest of the team.

"Got it?" she repeated.

"Got it."

She nodded, feeling a little silly but glad that she'd set some boundaries. It made her feel more confident, more in control.

"What all did Larry and Tim say?"

The earlier disappointment that she'd felt after speaking to them settled over her again like a dark cloud. "Larry had definitely been drinking. At first, I thought that was a good sign, that I was right and he'd been at the bar with the others. That maybe Tim ended up being the DD for everyone. But once I cut through his slurring, he admitted he'd left shortly after I had. Tim said much the same thing. They were both supposed to come up here, to Hawkins Ridge, in the morning, to do another exercise. The same exercise Dillon told me about before I left."

"Okay. Donna? Give me a minute alone inside, okay? I just want to have a quick look around while you phone this in."

"You think there could be more bodies, don't you? We were so focused on Randy that we didn't look around."

He was shaking his head before she finished. "No. It's a small barn. I don't think we could have missed another body, even in our peripheral vision. But I still want to see whether there are any obvious signs that anyone else was in there earlier. Okay? Will you wait right here?"

She nodded, even though she had no intention of waiting. She understood his concern for her welfare, for her peace of mind. After all, these people were her friends. But as she watched him head into the barn, sweeping his flashlight back and forth across the floor, she also understood that she couldn't cower away from her duty as a police officer. And there was something she needed to check out before the barn was turned over to the crime scene techs.

After calling the station, she hurried inside and was kneeling beside Randy's body when Blake finished his inspection and saw her. He rushed over, stopping just short of touching her this time.

"Donna. Don't. Please."

She had already pulled on a pair of latex gloves. Like most detectives she knew, she always kept a pair in her pocket for emergencies. This definitely qualified.

"I've already called the station," she assured him while she finished adjusting the gloves. "One of the patrolmen is going to come up here to secure the scene until the techs arrive. Another will call Maryville to borrow their M.E., or get old Doc Brookes to play medical examiner if the Maryville one isn't available. I didn't say who the victim was, though. I didn't want that to get out until I can notify Randy's mom. This is going to devastate her. He's single, an only child. And she's a widow. I'll probably get my mom to go over there and sit with her."

"That sounds like a wonderful idea, having your mom help out. I wouldn't have thought of that. Donna, what are you doing?"

"Checking something really quick before we go. Did you see any signs that the others were in here?"

"No. What exactly do you think you have to check?"

She was about to answer him, but her breath caught in her throat when she finally, for the first time since entering the barn, looked fully at Randy's body splayed out across the floor. A deep sadness welled up inside her. She was the oldest of three sisters, but had never felt deprived over not having any brothers. Her fellow detectives, her SWAT teammates, were her brothers. Randy more so, because he was so sweet-natured. But she couldn't give in to her grief. Not yet. Once she started crying, she might never stop. The best thing she could do for him right now was to engage her brain, not her emotions. She needed to study him objectively, as a victim, and soak in all the information she could glean from his injuries, which were, sadly, extensive.

"Donna."

"He didn't go quietly, did he?"

His gaze shifted to the body. "No. He didn't. He put up a good fight."

Randy lay on his back, his arms and legs akimbo, his unseeing eyes staring up at the rafters. Green eyes, the color of spring, she'd always teased him. They were his best feature. She couldn't believe she'd never look into those smiling eyes again.

His shirt was saturated with what had to be blood. It was reddish bronze, definitely not the bright red from their paintball guns. Blood had pooled faintly beneath the skin just below his eyes, revealing cellular damage, probably from being hit with a fist. If he'd survived long enough for bruises to fully form, the shadows would be black and purple shiners.

"Let's hope that he scraped a boatload of

DNA off the bastard and their profile is in the system already," she said. "From the looks of his shirt, I'd say he's been cut somehow—not necessarily stabbed—in addition to being shot. I count four bullet holes."

"Five. There's one on his leg, too. His right calf."

She had to fight to keep her breathing steady as she noted the fifth hole. His pants were soaked around the entry point, like his shirt. He'd been shot in the leg before his heart stopped pumping. Which meant he'd suffered.

Oh, Randy. Sweet, sweet Randy. How did this happen to you?

"Now can we go?" Blake asked, respecting her earlier insistence that he not pick her up again, even though it looked like it was killing him not to. He was a take-charge kind of man, probably not used to having to restrain his protective instincts.

"Soon. Did you bring your phone?"

He frowned. "Yes. Why?"

"I need you to photograph Randy's right hand before I pull that piece of paper out of it."

She'd laid her flashlight down on the ground, aimed toward Randy's hand. Blake looked down, his face mirroring surprise. He must not have noticed the paper earlier.

She could see the conflicting emotions in

his expression. They both knew they shouldn't touch the body, or anything around it. They should leave the evidence collection to the crime scene techs and the medical examiner. But there was a lot more at stake here than just bringing Randy's killer to justice. There were four more missing people who needed to be found before it was too late.

If it wasn't too late already.

The piece of paper clutched in Randy's hand could be the clue they needed to save their friends' lives. And the hours they'd have to wait for the techs and M.E. before they learned what was on that piece of paper were hours they couldn't afford to wait.

He glanced toward the barn doors, in the direction of the parking area. Then he pulled out his phone. "All right." He didn't sound happy with his decision as he raised the phone to snap the first picture. "But as soon as we see what he's holding, we put it back, exactly the way we found it."

"Agreed."

After snapping half a dozen pictures of Randy's hand from different angles, he nodded.

She leaned forward and carefully uncurled his fingers, while Blake continued to snap more pictures of the body.

"Full rigor hasn't set in yet," she told him. "He hasn't been dead very long."

They both glanced toward the open barn doors.

"We're excellent targets in here with our flashlights lighting us up for a shooter," he said. "Proverbial sitting ducks."

"I was thinking the same thing. I'll hurry."

After gently working the paper free, she unfolded it. Blue cursive writing was scrawled across the white square, about a third the size of a typical sheet of notebook paper. There were only two sentences, neat and precise, as if the author had taken a painstaking amount of time to get them just so.

This wasn't a spur-of-the-moment murder. It was planned.

"What's it say?" Blake asked. "I can't make it out."

Her hand shook as she held it up in the air.

His jaw tightening was the only indication that he'd read it. He snapped several more pictures. "You know what this means, don't you?"

She nodded. "We need the cavalry on this. But they won't help us without knowing the special circumstances. And that means revealing that we read the note. We're trapped in a catch-22."

"It's only a trap if we try to wiggle out of it.

Fold the paper and put it back exactly the way we found it. We'll come clean, admit that we touched it, but that we used gloves and tried to leave it the same way that we found it so we could maintain the integrity of the evidence. Then we'll face the consequences."

"The consequences are that we'll be removed from the case. No way am I going to let that happen. After reading what that note said, are you seriously going to stand there judging me and say that you wished we had waited hours for a medical examiner to give us a report? Really?"

He blew out a deep breath. "Okay, okay. You're right. In this instance, it's good that we read it. But covering it up after the fact—"

"Is exactly what we *both* agreed to do *before* we read it. You aren't exactly pristine in this little endeavor. So, are we in this together or not?"

Without waiting for his reply, she refolded the note, leaving both sentences clearly visible instead of hidden like they were before. Then she slid the edge between Randy's thumb and pointer finger to keep the paper from falling. "There. Anyone looking at the body can clearly see what the killer wrote. There's no reason to admit that's not how it looked when we got here."

"What if the way the killer folded and staged

the presentation is significant to the crime? It could be an important clue to figuring out his identity."

"We'll pursue that angle on our own. If we find it's truly significant, we'll figure out a way to let others know."

Disapproval seemed to seep from every pore as he frowned down at her like an archangel ready to release his wrath.

"Let it go, Blake. I'm not going to screw up this investigation. But I'm not going to be kicked off it either."

He looked like he wanted to argue more, but the sound of a siren in the distance had him swearing beneath his breath instead. "We need to get out of here. Respected police officer or not, you're about to be tossed over my shoulder and hauled out of this barn if you don't get moving."

"Meaning you're going to let this go?"

He gave her a curt nod and offered a hand to help her up.

Relieved that he'd given in, she took his hand and climbed to her feet.

"Don't forget the gloves." He motioned toward her hands.

She rolled the latex down her wrists, turning them inside out before shoving them into her back pocket.

He shook his head. "They're lumpy now. Someone might notice and ask about it. I don't want you to get fired, too. I'll put them in *my* pocket. If anyone finds out, it won't matter. They can't fire me twice."

"No." She grabbed the gloves and shoved them down her bra. "No one's getting fired. Including you."

His eyes had widened as he watched her hide the gloves. Now he cleared his throat and seemed to have difficulty lifting his gaze to look her in the eye again. "What do you mean, that includes me?"

"Detective Waters? Detective Sullivan?" The words were muted, coming from a considerable distance away. The uniformed patrolman she'd spoken to on the phone must have arrived and was looking for them.

"I'm saying," she said, lowering her voice, "that the only other person here who knows that Dillon fired you is me. And I sure don't want to work this case by myself. I need your help. You can't help me if you're a civilian."

He pulled her to a halt. "In addition to tampering with evidence—"

"I wouldn't call it tampering, exactly. We discovered something extremely important and made sure it can be shared and acted upon quickly."

"In addition to tampering," he repeated, "now you want me to lie and pretend I wasn't fired?"

"If that's what it takes to save our friends, our coworkers, then absolutely, yes. Lie."

She was all about having a conscience. But this was a heck of a time for him to be wrestling with it. Again.

She put her hands on her hips. "Seriously? You *really* have to think about this one?"

Her phone buzzed against her hip. She blew out an impatient breath and took the call. "Detective Waters." She listened for a moment, then said, "Yes, I heard you calling to us, Officer Lynch. We're heading toward the parking area now."

She ended the call and shoved her phone back into her pocket. "Well, Blake? You've had time to think about it. Not that you should need it."

He cursed viciously. "Okay. I'll do it. But I don't like it."

"That much is obvious." She narrowed her eyes in warning. "I can't believe you even hesitated."

They started off again toward where Officer Lynch was waiting.

"We're heading down a slippery slope," he gritted out. "One lie always leads to another. This could get really complicated, really fast, and jeopardize the court case later on. It might blow up in our faces and have all kinds of un-foreseen repercussions."

"I'm not worried about a court case or reper-cussions. I'm worried about my friends' lives."

"Your *friend* Dillon wanted me off the force. I'm trying to do right by him."

"Yeah, well. Do right by helping me save his life. You can ask him to forgive you later."

He rolled his eyes.

A few minutes later, they stepped out of the woods beside Chris's blue pickup. She motioned for the patrolman who was standing by his car, bar lights flashing red and blue.

"There's one more thing we have to decide," she whispered.

"Wonderful." Sarcasm practically dripped off his words. "Can't wait to hear it."

She pressed the flat of her hand against his chest, her throat suddenly tight. "How are we going to break the news that a lunatic murdered Randy and is holding three more members of our team and the police chief hostage?"

Chapter Seven

Blake headed up the long concrete walkway beside Donna, his flashlight off even though it was close to two in the morning. The outside of Mrs. Carter's cottage was lit up like midday, with security lights framing both sides of the path and carriage lamps all across the wall of the front porch. Motion sensors had flooded the front and side yards with light the moment he parked his truck in the gravel out front.

Even now he could see lights coming on inside, probably because the motion sensors were hooked up to some kind of alert that had awakened the owner. Knowing cops in general and their intense need to protect their loved ones from the evil they encountered on a daily basis, Blake figured it was a safe bet that Randy was the one who was responsible for all these gadgets at his mother's home.

"How long before your mother gets here to sit with Mrs. Carter?" he asked.

"Probably five or ten minutes." She stopped. "We should wait. What was I thinking? I can't do this on my own. I can't tell her... I can't do this."

She turned back toward the truck, but he grasped her shoulders and gently forced her to face him. "Donna, you can do this. You're not alone. I'm with you, and I'm not going anywhere."

She shook her head. "You don't understand. Randy was like a brother to me. I've known him my whole life. We went to school together, from pre-K on. We went to prom together because neither of us had dates. It was one of the best nights of my life, because we were two friends just having fun, you know? No pressure. No weird goodnight kiss or worries that someone was going to want more than I wanted to give. He lived in this house his whole life. When... when we were little, we played in the backyard. He'd steal my dolls, and I'd steal his Matchbox cars." She sniffed, her eyes sparkling with unshed tears. "How do I tell her he's gone? I have to wait, let my mother tell her."

He slowly shook his head. "We can't wait. Mrs. Carter is standing in the doorway right now, watching us through the storm door."

Her eyes widened, and she shot a quick look

toward the house. "Blake, you have to tell her. I'm sorry. Let me go. I—"

The creak of the storm door shattered the quiet. "Donna? Sweetie? Is that you?" Mrs. Carter stepped out onto the porch, tying the sash around her blue terry cloth robe. Matching blue fuzzy slippers protected her feet.

Donna gave Blake a pleading look.

He squeezed her shoulders. "It will be better coming from someone who knows her, who loves her, who loved her son."

"Donna? Who's that with you, dear?"

She drew a deep breath. Then another.

"Donna?" Blake asked.

"Okay. Okay. I can do this."

He dropped his hands from her shoulders.

When she turned to face the house, she pasted a smile on her face. "Mrs. Carter, so sorry to bother you at this insane hour of the morning." She hurried up onto the porch and took Randy's mother's hands in hers.

Blake climbed the steps and stood a few feet back, waiting.

Mrs. Carter stared up into Donna's eyes, her faded blue eyes searching Donna's. Like all law-enforcement family members, this woman was no stranger to the police life and had to know that a 2:00 a.m. visit from the police—without her son present—wasn't a social visit.

"Hurt or dead?" Mrs. Carter's voice shook as she waited for Donna's reply.

Donna slowly shook her head. "Oh, Mrs. Carter. I'm so, so sorry."

The elderly woman let out a small cry and started to crumple. Blake rushed forward and caught her in his arms before she could fall. Donna pulled open the door, tears freely rolling down her cheeks now as Blake carried the woman inside.

After settling her onto a baby-blue flower-patterned couch, he tucked one of the throw pillows beneath her head. Donna covered her with a cream-colored afghan that she'd grabbed from a side chair.

The old woman's eyes were closed, but she wasn't asleep. Tears streamed down her face, and her shoulders shook with silent sobs. Donna settled on the floor in front of the couch, holding one of the woman's hands while she gently stroked her hair and whispered soothing words.

Not sure how to help, Blake glanced around the small room. It was neat as a pin, as was the kitchen, visible through an arched opening.

"Tea. You should make her some tea," a feminine voice called out from somewhere behind him.

He turned to see a woman standing on the porch with gray-streaked blond hair cut to frame a face that could have been a twin to Donna's, except for the twenty or so years separating them.

Blake hurried to open the door for her. "Mrs. Waters, pleasure to meet you. I'm Detective—"

"I know who you are." She smiled as if to soften her words. "Call me Miranda, Blake. Do you know how to make hot tea?"

"Yes, ma'am."

Her brows arched up.

"Yes, Miranda," he corrected.

She smiled and patted the side of his face. "She takes two sugar cubes and a dash of cream. I take mine black." She gave him a shooing motion and hurried to the couch, where she hugged Donna. She then took a seat on the coffee table and took Mrs. Carter's other hand in her own.

Feeling relieved to have something to do, Blake went into the kitchen and tried to remember how to make hot tea. It had been years since he'd seen his mom make it, and thankfully it was as easy as he remembered. Randy's mother was obviously quite fond of the stuff. She had a teakettle on the stove, which he filled with water and turned on to boil. A teapot and service sat on the counter, along with an assortment of tea bags, sugar cubes in a delicate bowl and a tiny empty pitcher that he guessed was for the cream.

After searching through the refrigerator, he gave up figuring out what container might hold cream and went for the milk instead.

"Need any help?"

He turned with the quart of milk poised to pour into the little pitcher. Donna stood in the opening, shaking her head when she saw the milk.

"Half-and-half," she said, taking the milk from him and heading to the refrigerator. After exchanging the quart of milk for a pint-size container that looked like a miniature milk carton, she filled up the little pitcher. "There. All ready, except for the water."

"Thanks," he said as she replaced the container of half-and-half in the refrigerator.

"You did great on your own," she said. "Just figured I'd check on you. I don't recall you being a tea drinker."

"Not my thing," he admitted. "But I've suffered through a few cups in my day. Mom laced tea with whiskey and honey when we had sore throats. The only reason I gave in was the whiskey."

She smiled. "I would have done the same thing. I never liked tea either."

The kettle on the stove started to whistle. Blake moved toward it, but Donna gently pushed him out of the way. "I've got this." She turned off the stove and poured hot water into the teapot. She added a second cup to the tray. "There. Mom and Mrs. Carter can exchange stories about Randy over an entire pot of tea. They're already talking about the silly things he used to do as a kid. Mom's a miracle worker. I'm glad she came."

He glanced past her, relieved to see that Randy's mom was sitting up now, beside Donna's mom on the couch. Their heads were close together as they talked, and Donna's mom was holding the other woman's hand.

"She seems like a no-nonsense lady, your mom," he said. "Strong and kind. Like you."

"I don't know how strong I am right now. I'm barely holding it together." She waved toward the tea tray. "Want to carry that for me? Not that I can't do it. But I'm not so much a feminist that I'm threatened by letting a guy do the heavy lifting if one's around."

In answer, he carried the tray into the other room.

The two women on the couch barely seemed to notice him as he left the tray on the coffee table. They spoke in low whispers, and he distinctly heard Mrs. Carter mention Randy's name while smiling through her tears.

"We're going to head out, Mom, Mrs. Carter."

Donna hugged both women, whispered something to Randy's mom, then nodded at Blake.

They quietly made their way outside and down the steps. Blake waited until they were at his truck before he asked, "Are you sure you don't want to stay here with your mom? I can handle things back at the station."

She shook her head but didn't say anything as she climbed into the passenger side.

They'd just rounded a corner, the cottage disappearing from sight in the rearview mirror, when she grabbed her door handle. "Pull over."

He looked through the windshield but didn't see whatever had her alarmed. "I don't see anything. What's the—"

"Pull over. Now."

He yanked the steering wheel and jerked the truck to a stop on the shoulder of the road. "Donna—"

She threw the passenger door open and barely made it into the bushes before she started retching.

Blake jumped out of the truck, leaving the engine running and the headlights on to light the way as he rushed toward her.

"Don't," she gasped. "Leave me alone." Her whole body shuddered as she retched again.

Ignoring her order, he crouched behind her and pulled her hair back from her face.

Apparently too sick to yell at him again, she threw up over and over, until she started to dry heave. When the storm finally passed, she shook her head and pushed his hands back, letting her hair fall around her face.

Blake moved to the side and gently tilted her chin to look at him. "Is it Randy? Or are you sick?"

She jerked her head back, forcing him to lower his hand. She blinked several times, drawing quick, shallow breaths. "Sh-she… Mrs. Carter, she asked me…" She shook her head and swiped at the tears now flowing down her cheeks. "I knew he was dead. I mean, I saw his broken body, saw the blood. But I didn't… I don't think it hit me that he's really gone, that he's…dead…until his mother asked me to help her plan his funeral."

Her shoulders shook as sobs suddenly racked her body, even worse than the dry heaves from moments earlier.

Blake swore and scooped her onto his lap. She stiffened at first, but then threw her arms around him and buried her head against his chest. His heart seemed to crack as he listened to her crying, felt her hot wet tears soak into his shirt. If her friend's murderer had appeared in front of him right then, Blake would have ripped the man's throat out with his bare hands for causing Donna such pain.

He rocked her against him, gently rubbing her back until she quieted. Then, as if she'd suddenly realized where she was, she shoved at his chest.

"What are you doing?" Her eyes widened. Then she jerked her face to the side and cupped a hand over her mouth. "Oh, my gosh. I have to smell terrible."

"I don't care how you smell." He lifted her in his arms and stood.

Still keeping one hand cupped over her mouth, she said, "I told you not to carry me. I can walk perfectly fine."

"Your whole body is shaking, and you're way too stubborn to admit when you need help."

In spite of her protests, she didn't try to push herself out of his arms; she let him carry her the rest of the way to the truck. After settling her in the passenger side, he reached for the seat belt.

She tried to grab it out of his hand, but he simply finished clicking it into place. Then he snagged a clean rag and a bottle of water from the box of supplies he kept behind the seat.

He held them out to her without a word.

"Thank you," she said grudgingly as she took them.

"You're welcome."

He slowly walked around the back of the truck, giving her privacy and enough time to rinse out her mouth. When he hopped into the cab and shut his door, she pulled hers shut, too, and looked straight ahead through the windshield. Her cheeks were flushed, and he knew her well enough to realize that she was probably embarrassed that he'd been there to witness her being sick. Which of course was silly. She could be sick in front of him a hundred times, and it wouldn't bother him. What would bother him was if she needed him and he couldn't be there to help her.

He shook his head at himself.

Ever since Donna had walked into that bar, braving the stink and the worst dregs of humanity because she cared enough about him to try to save his job, he'd been off-kilter. The feelings he'd worked so hard to ignore were boiling too close to the surface—especially after finding Randy murdered. He kept picturing what might have happened if he hadn't gotten fired, if Donna hadn't come after him. Would she have been the one who had been killed? Would the killer have chosen her as his victim instead of Randy? Just imagining her lying there, broken, bleeding, sent a cold chill straight through him.

"Blake? Are *you* okay?"

Her question had him forcing a smile. "Of

course." Since she was staring at him so intensely, as if trying to figure out what he was thinking, he threw her a curveball. "I'll have to take a rain check on taking you to bed. Maybe until all this is over. You know, since I went against your dictate and carried you again." He gave her an outrageous wink.

Her eyes widened. Then she started laughing. The delightful sound was like a balm to his soul, somehow giving him the strength he needed to lock away his ridiculous emotions and face the task ahead—the investigation, and the search for their friends.

He put the truck into drive and headed down the road. A few minutes later, he stopped at an intersection. "Back to the station? Or do you want me to drop you off at your house to get some sleep?"

She shook her head. "I can't sleep. Not yet. Not until I know…something, anything, that can shed some light on what's going on."

A half hour passed before they pulled into the empty parking lot of the stand-alone building that was several miles outside town, surrounded by woods. According to what the chief had told him, the idea when the police station was built was that the town would eventually grow out this far and surround it. So, rather than use the more expensive land back in Destiny, the station had been constructed pretty much in the middle of nowhere. That was a decade ago. And Destiny, Tennessee, showed no signs of growing outside its current boundaries.

They were heading up the walkway to the front glass doors when she stopped him with a hand on his arm.

"You never saw me cry," she said. "And you sure never saw me throw up."

"I don't even know what you're talking about."

Her expression mirrored relief. "Thank you."

They headed up the walk again. When they reached the doors, he pulled one of them open for her. "Donna?"

She hesitated and looked up at him. "Yes?"

"Crying, or being sick with grief over a loved one, neither of those makes you weak. They make you human. You're one of the strongest people I know. Nothing that happened today changed that."

She blinked, then cleared her throat and stepped inside. They'd only gone a few feet when she glanced at him over her shoulder. "Blake?"

"Yes?"

"Thank you. For everything." Without waiting for his reply, she strode through the squad room, grabbed a small toiletry bag out of her desk and hurried down the back hallway to the bathroom.

Chapter Eight

At 4:00 a.m. on a typical Sunday, there were one, maybe two, Destiny, Tennessee, police officers on duty. This Sunday, there were ten, plus a dozen state police. Every law-enforcement officer in the county who wasn't already on assignment had shown up in answer to Donna's calls, eager to help their fellow officers. Even some local civilians, awakened by her infamous call tree, were pitching in any way they could.

But only Blake and Donna were at the police station.

Everyone else was either helping collect evidence at Hawkins Ridge or scouring the county for potential witnesses.

Blake rubbed the stubble on his jaw and leaned back in his desk chair, looking around the nearly empty squad room. The freestanding building had only one entrance and exit that opened directly into this room. A kitchenette ran along the wall to the right of the entrance.

Past that was the police chief's office and private bathroom. Along the back was a short hallway with two holding cells and the restroom the officers used. And to the left of the entrance was an interview room. The place was small, but efficient, and very quiet.

Too quiet.

He longed to be outside with everyone else, searching for clues. But since he and Donna were the only detectives left, here they sat, hunched over their keyboards in the last row of desks.

He rubbed his bleary eyes. One desk over, Donna was squinting at the computer monitor as if trying to focus.

Her shoulder-length blond hair was cut into a straight bob that gently curved around her face, giving her what Blake had always thought of as a pixie look, like a tiny magical fairy sent down to dwell among mortals. Or, at least, normally it curved around her face. Right now her hair was sticking up all around her head. The blouse she'd so carefully tucked into her jeans before they went up to Hawkins Ridge was hanging out in the back now, severely wrinkled. What little eye makeup she'd had on hours ago was now smeared, reminding him of a raccoon.

He didn't think she'd ever looked more beautiful. Too bad they were coworkers and the chief frowned on dating among coworkers. Apparently Max had been a ladies' man around the station at one time, dating interns and wreaking havoc whenever the relationships eventually ended. Now that he was caught for good by his wife, Bex, things had settled down. But he'd pretty much ruined it for the rest of them. Which meant Blake had to work extra hard at not letting Donna know that he'd grown to care about her a whole lot more than he should over the past few months. As smart and beautiful and fun as she was to be around, it wasn't easy.

He silently cursed himself for even thinking about something so unimportant in light of the case they were working on. He must be more tired than he'd realized, sitting here, mooning over Donna when he should be trying to find their missing coworkers. Looking at her now, seeing how pale and drawn her face was, he realized she had to be just as worn out as he felt. Maybe they both needed a break, so they could refocus on the case.

"You're exhausted," he announced, rolling his chair next to hers. "We both are. We should go home and get some sleep."

She blinked as if coming out of a trance, her fingers growing still on the keyboard. "What time is it?"

"A little after four."

"A little after four," she repeated, staring at the screen with a haunted look in her eyes. "Did you know that most people who are abducted are killed within the first three hours? We've failed them, Blake. They've been out there for far longer than that."

"That statistic applies to juveniles, not adults. And it typically involves pedophiles. We're dealing with something entirely different here. Let's focus on solving Randy's murder. We're well within the golden forty-eight-hour window, where most homicides are solved. Focus on that. We find his killer, we find the others alive and well and bring them home."

She shook her head. "I'm doing everything I can, but it doesn't feel like enough."

"You're forgetting something really important here."

She finally turned her head and met his gaze. "What's that?"

"This killer didn't kidnap just anyone. He kidnapped some of the most well-trained, intelligent, savvy cops I've ever met. I've worked with a lot of officers, so that's saying something. We're still a team here. You and I are working this case from the outside. But Dillon, Chris, Max and the chief are working it from the inside. That's an impressive group. Together, there's no telling what they'll get done.

It wouldn't surprise me if they came walking in here in the next few hours with their kidnapper in handcuffs."

The corner of her mouth lifted in a smile. "I can totally picture that."

"Good. Hold on to that image and don't get discouraged. We're going to find this guy and bring our team home."

"Guy. One killer. I don't see it. You said yourself, Dillon and the others are an impressive team, formidable even. There's no way that one person could have killed Randy and taken the rest of them hostage. We're looking at a group of bad guys here."

"I won't argue with you there. I've been thinking the same thing."

She swiveled her chair toward him and started ticking off salient points on her fingers. "There's a lack of tire tracks. A meticulous note that had to be written ahead of time and brought to the scene. Transportation. Someone had to work that out ahead of time—a truck or van, something that could hold all our guys. And they sure as heck had to have a lot of firepower and manpower to make our men get into that vehicle without fighting them. A fight would have left obvious signs of a struggle at the scene, which there wasn't. All of that speaks to this being a large, well-planned operation."

Crossing her arms, she leaned back in her chair. "When you hear about criminals being highly organized, well planned, well resourced and willing to go after cops—a SWAT team for goodness' sake— what does that make you think?"

He didn't even have to think about it. "Drugs."

She nodded. "Exactly. That's what I'm thinking, too. But we haven't had any major drug cases in this county in years. The worst we've had is a few farmers growing pot plants out in their tobacco fields, hoping no one would notice a few Mary Janes mixed in here and there. But that was for personal use. This is way bigger than that."

"You're thinking methamphetamines."

"Possibly. Or some new exotic drug being manufactured in a homegrown lab. There's always something new out on the streets in big cities. You worked in Knoxville. Did you see any of that?"

"I worked homicides, so I didn't have much firsthand exposure to the drug operations going on. But there was enough crossover in the murder cases I worked to get a feel for it. I've still got a few contacts there. I can call them up in a few hours when they're in and put out some feelers, see if there are some groups looking to spread out into a rural county that might be behind this. But that doesn't feel right either. A major drug-running operation wouldn't want to draw attention by taking police officers captive. If the cops came across their lab or something like that, sure, there could be a bloodbath, a shoot-out. But that's not what we have here."

"The note," she said.

"The note. If this is drugs, why kidnap cops and leave a ransom note? That's the complete opposite of lying low and trying not to be caught. Whoever is behind this wants attention."

She shook her head and fisted her hands in frustration. "Not drugs, then. So what is it?"

"I didn't say it wasn't drugs. That still fits the well-funded, well-resourced side of this. But maybe the goal isn't to hide something. Maybe the goal is to send a message."

"What's the message? We don't have any ongoing drug investigations right now. So it's not like someone needs to threaten us to back off." She grabbed a small stack of manila folders from the far corner of her desk and plopped them on the corner closest to Blake. "We have three open investigations in Destiny. Two are typical local stuff—petty theft—and we know who's responsible. It's just a matter of gathering enough evidence to go to court. The third is the only serious one—"

"Our John Doe murder last month."

She nodded. "A stranger, a hitchhiker found shot multiple times, his body left lying in a ditch. He was in a remote section of the county near a two-lane highway that mostly only locals use. No witnesses. No tire tracks. No clues other than the bullet Doc Brookes dug out of the body—nine-millimeter. The backpack the hiker wore had typical hiker stuff in it. Best we can figure, he was hiking in the Smokies and decided to go off-trail and ended up here. Until we figure out who he is or find someone who actually saw him before he was killed, we're at an impasse. But no matter how I look at it, there's nothing about his murder that makes me think it could be part of what's going on here."

It was Blake's turn to count off points on his fingers. "Shot multiple times. No witnesses. No tire tracks. Left dead in a remote area. Sound familiar?"

Her eyes widened. "Randy."

He shrugged. "Maybe. Maybe not. But at the very least, I'm thinking a fresh look at John Doe's murder is warranted."

"Agreed." She flipped open the folder.

Blake flipped it closed.

"What are you doing?" She frowned at him.

"It's almost four thirty. Neither of us has slept in almost twenty-four hours. We're running on empty. This—" he tapped the folder "—can wait. We won't be any good to anyone if we don't get at least a couple of hours of shut-eye."

Her shoulders slumped. "You're right. I can barely see straight. But until someone comes back to hold down the fort, we can't just leave."

"We're not doing anyone any good in our current conditions."

She shook her head, her mouth drawn into a mutinous line. "I'm not ready to stop. Not yet. I can't bear the idea of no one working the investigation while we lie around and do nothing."

"It's not nothing. It's recharging our batteries so we can be useful again."

Her silence was his answer. The only way he was getting her out of here right now was if he picked her up and carried her. And he'd already learned what she thought about that plan. Unless he was her lover carrying her to bed, of course. He swallowed and forced his tired, out-of-control thoughts not to wander in that direction again.

"What time is the cavalry supposed to get here?" he asked.

"They didn't say. But with an officer down, and four missing, I sure expected they'd be here by now. Especially since the Knoxville FBI field office is less than an hour away."

He picked up the folder. "Tell you what. While we wait for them, let me poke around a little more on the John Doe case. I'll expand the cross-check against missing persons to within a hundred-mile radius, see if something new pops up. You're working on the timelines for our team, right? How close are they to being done?"

"I could use a few more hours to close some gaps."

"All right," he allowed. "We'll give it a few more hours. If they're not here by six—"

"Seven. We'll give them until seven."

He blew out a long breath. "Okay. Seven. If they're not here by seven, we get one of your call-tree buddies to man the phones while we go home and get at least a few hours of sleep before coming back. Agreed?"

She looked reluctant, but even sitting here, talking to him, she was struggling to keep her eyes open. He wasn't even sure she could make it until seven, but he was trying to placate her. Finally, she nodded and turned back to her keyboard.

"I'm going to need some coffee." She started typing and arched a brow. "It's your turn."

He smiled. "Black as always?"

"Cream and sugar to cut the bitterness, unless you're making a fresh pot?"

Her hopeful look had him smiling again. "One fresh pot of coffee coming up."

He crossed to the left of the glass-walled

entrance, with its double doors, to where the long counter boasted a microwave, a coffeepot and an assortment of snacks, since they didn't have a vending machine. The mini fridge underneath the counter held sodas and water. The mini freezer beside it held an assortment of baked goods that Dillon's wife, Ashley, restocked every now and then, so they'd always have something good to nibble on. He set a couple of trays of muffins on the counter, figuring they'd be thawed out around breakfast time for whoever was in the station come sunup.

As he went through the motions of putting a fresh filter and grounds in the coffee maker, he called over his shoulder, "When will Ashley and the others be back from the cruise? We're going to have to notify them about what's going on. And interview them, too, in case they can contribute to the timeline."

"The ship docks in Miami today, around five in the afternoon. They're going shopping and taking in the sights. Then they'll fly into Nashville International Airport tomorrow. From there, they'll take a puddle-jumper to McGhee Tyson. I figure they'll get there close to noon. Since it's just a few minutes down the road, you and I could meet them when they get off the plane. I don't want to risk them hearing about this from any well-meaning friends in Destiny who don't realize they haven't heard the news yet. And I don't see the point of calling them now, ruining the end of their vacation just to tell them we don't have any leads. I'd rather hope and pray we find our team, safe and sound, before we even have to tell their families what happened."

Blake wasn't so sure that he agreed with her plan. He'd rather wake them and see if they knew anything that could help build the timeline. But since Donna was the one working on that timeline, he'd trust her to know if there were any gaps, anything she needed to corroborate. There were plenty of avenues of investigation they could explore right now. He was itching to get his hands on any information from the crime scene. And the autopsy might give them a DNA link to their killer. Hopefully Doc Brookes or the Maryville M.E. had the body at his office by now and was busy looking for clues.

He leaned against the counter, resting his eyes while listening to the tapping of Donna's fingers on her keyboard and the soothing sound of coffee pouring into the pot. It seemed like only a few seconds had passed when the machine beeped, letting him know the pot was full, ten cups ready for consumption. He must have dozed off standing up. He shook his head and poured them both cups before returning to their desks at the back of the room.

Donna murmured her thanks and took a deep, appreciative sniff before drinking some down.

Blake sipped his then set it aside as he noted what was beside Donna's keyboard. "The chief's planner? Where did you find that?"

She yawned and set her cup down. "In his office, of course. I grabbed it while you were snoozing by the counter. You snore, by the way."

Since no one had ever told him that before, he figured she was teasing. He sure hoped so, anyway. "I searched his office when we first got here. I didn't see a planner."

"Did you check his wall safe?"

"Wall safe?"

"Behind his desk, to the left of the window, hidden by that hideous deer head he hung up last summer. Not that he even hunts. I think his nephew gave it to him. You've never seen him use the safe?"

"I'm not exactly his confidant."

Her mouth tightened. "Yeah, sorry about that. When this is over, maybe we can all have a kumbaya moment together and become a real team."

He didn't bother to remind her that he'd been fired and would never be part of her team again. Their current pretense was only until they could find their missing peers. As soon as Dillon was back—and Blake refused to believe that he wouldn't be back—Dillon would tell him to get out. Which was yet another reason not to allow himself to pursue his attraction to Donna. There was no sense in trying to start a relationship when he'd soon be moving to another county, maybe even another state if that was what it took to find a job.

"The combination is the chief's wife's birthday, by the way. Two digits each for the month, day and year, just in case you ever need to get in there. The main reason he has the thing is to keep his spare gun locked up. He doesn't like to stow it in the gun cabinet with our rifles."

He gave her a curt nod and returned to his desk, coffee in hand. He didn't bother to remind her that he didn't know Claire Thornton's birth date, or that the chief wouldn't want him knowing the combination. That last part was a no-brainer, since he'd never even told Blake that he had a safe.

They worked in silence, taking turns getting each other coffee refills, desperately needing the caffeine to stay awake.

"How's the timeline coming?" he asked, when the wall clock above the front doors had inched past six thirty.

"It's about ready to review, actually." She motioned for him to join her.

He rolled his chair over, and she explained the setup of her worksheet, with a tab for each of the team members—including one for Randy.

Sounds from outside had both of them looking up. A group of seven men and women in dark-colored business suits, with crisp white button-up dress shirts and ties, headed up the walkway toward the front doors. Every one of them was holding a briefcase.

"Looks like the cavalry has finally arrived." Blake stood. "Only the feds know how to match their business suits so well that you can't tell them apart."

Donna let out a sigh and walked with him toward the front. "The chief would hate that I called the feds for help. Things didn't turn out so well the last time an FBI agent came out here to work with us on a case."

"Really? What happened?"

"He was murdered."

Chapter Nine

Donna tried not to let it bother her, or at least not let it show that it bothered her, when she let Supervisory Special Agent Richard Grant into the chief's office. Once the fellow FBI agents that Grant had brought with him were all there at the same time as the Destiny P.D. officers and the state police, the place would be overflowing. It only made sense to give Grant this office. But it still felt like she was being a traitor to her boss.

He *really* didn't like the feds.

She glanced at Blake, standing next to the door as if he couldn't wait to get back to his desk. She couldn't blame him. Even taking time to give a tour of their tiny police station meant taking time away from the investigation, time they couldn't afford to waste. And in spite of the fact that they were both asleep on their feet, there were things they wanted to wrap up before being forced to get some shut-eye.

Grant set his briefcase on the desk and looked around the rather large office with its private bathroom. "Thank you for offering your chief's office for the duration. Looks like we could fit a few small tables in here and some folding chairs to accommodate my direct reports."

He indicated the three special agents who'd come inside with him. She'd already forgotten their names.

"Do you have anything like that?" he asked. "Folding tables? Chairs?"

She motioned toward the window behind the desk. "There's a storage building out back where the maintenance guys keep their tools and lawn equipment for when they make trips out here. There might be some folding tables and chairs too, not sure. But the chief never throws anything away. Every time we get a new piece of furniture or equipment, the old one goes out there, broken or not. Key's in the top desk drawer. Help yourself. Any office supplies you need—paper, pens, that sort of thing—should be in the file cabinets that run along the wall by the interview room. Those aren't locked."

He opened the top drawer, rummaged through it and pulled out the key she'd indicated. "Joel, Colin, why don't you see if there's anything out back we can use? It's going to be tight quarters around here, and it would be nice if everyone at least has somewhere to sit."

"Will do."

The one he'd called Colin—his name was Colin Lopez, she remembered now—took the key and headed to the door with Joel in tow. Blake opened the door for them and nodded as they stepped out of the office.

"Stacy," Grant said, indicating the remaining agent. "Can you give me a few moments alone with Detective Waters and Detective Sullivan please?"

"Of course." She paused beside Donna. "I'm terribly sorry for your loss, Detective. I'm Special Agent Stacy Bell, in case you forgot. If there's anything I can do for you, please let me know. We've both got the same goal. Catch the bad guys and save the good guys."

"Um, thank you." Donna shook the agent's hand, surprised at her little speech.

Stacy paused beside Blake and offered her condolences to him, as well, before leaving the office.

Blake shrugged when Donna looked at him. He obviously didn't know what to make of that speech either.

Grant sat behind the desk and motioned toward the two chairs in front of it.

"Detectives, won't you both sit down so we

can discuss things more in-depth than the earlier summary you gave me?"

Donna slowly lowered herself into one of the chairs, feeling as confused as Blake looked as he closed the door. He settled into the chair beside hers. They hadn't given Grant a *summary* when he arrived. They'd told him every single detail they could remember. Well, except for two details that she had no intention of sharing—that she'd touched the note in Randy's hand and that Blake was technically a civilian.

"I'm not really sure what else you want to discuss," she said. "I think we told you everything. Unfortunately, we don't know very much yet. Which is why Blake and I would both like to get back to our desks to work on the investigation."

"Let's talk about the note that brought me and my team here."

He pulled a piece of paper out of his pocket and smoothed it out on top of the desk. It was a full sheet of paper, obviously a copy of the original that Randy had been holding. He read the words out loud.

"Instructions for ransom will follow. If you don't obey the instructions, the remaining members of your SWAT team will end up like this one."

"What's your take on the writing?" he asked.

Donna swallowed at the tightness in her throat. Her emotions were still too raw. She was barely holding herself together. "I'm not sure why you're asking me. I'm no handwriting expert. Isn't that the sort of thing you guys do?"

He smiled. "Yes, one of many things that we do. I have the original with an expert now, as a matter of fact. But time is critical. And I'm not from this area. I thought perhaps your instincts might be valuable in helping ferret out any clues about the author of the note."

She cleared her throat. "I see your point. Sorry. I'm running on empty, not thinking as clearly as usual. May I?"

"Please."

She took the note from him and leaned toward Blake so they could both study it. But her eyes felt like they were crossing trying to read the script and make out the letters. It was now seven thirty in the morning, which meant she was coming up on twenty-five hours without sleep.

"I can't even make the words focus." She handed the note to Blake. "What about you?"

He frowned down at the paper. "The obvious of course is that someone probably wrote this ahead of time. It's too perfect to have been scribbled at the scene. It's dirty and wet up on Hawkins Ridge from the storms that blew through yesterday afternoon. I remember the original paper was clean, crisp. Or at least, it looked crisp."

"Go on."

"It's not written in colloquial terms. It's formal— perfect grammar, punctuation. Almost too perfect."

Richard sat forward in his chair. "Too perfect?"

Blake handed him back the note. "It's as if someone is trying too hard not to make a mistake. I wonder if English might be their second language, so they referred to a grammar guide to get it just so. At any rate, I doubt they're from around here. That's not how we talk."

Donna smiled at him, but he wasn't sure why.

"Interesting angle. Anything else?" Richard asked.

"It refers to the SWAT team, but the chief isn't part of the SWAT team and he was taken, too. Plus, Donna and I are on the team and weren't there at the time the others were kidnapped. So any leads we pursue should be based on the intent, not what actually happened. I think the intent was to kidnap just the SWAT team, not the chief. Which takes him out of the equation as far as victimology is concerned." He shrugged. "Like Donna's, my mind isn't firing on all synapses right now. We've both been up all night. So I'm not sure what anything I just said really means, or if it matters in the investigation. I'll have to look at it fresh later."

Richard tapped the chief's favorite pen on top of the desk blotter. Donna wanted to snatch it away, tell him not to touch the chief's things. She had to curl her fingers against her palms to resist the juvenile impulse.

In the window behind Grant, she could see the two agents that he'd sent outside pulling things out of the storage building. She wanted to stop them, too. They were rummaging around in the chief's things, invading his privacy. And none of it was helping anyone find him, or the others.

"You mentioned that neither of you was on the ridge when the team disappeared," Grant said, breaking through her thoughts. "Why not?"

She blinked. Suddenly she realized that neither she nor Blake had discussed a cover story for this before the agents got here. The only reason that she wasn't there was that she wanted to find Blake and try to get him to apologize to Dillon and get his job back. If she admitted that, Blake would have to leave and quit working the case. What would happen to her? Did the FBI have any authority over her? She didn't think so.

"Detective Waters?"

Blake put his hand on hers and squeezed. "You probably haven't been up this late since college, huh?"

His words might have been teasing, but she read the seriousness in his eyes. He was trying to cover her hesitation, help her through it. But nothing was coming to her. Her mind had gone completely blank.

"It's my fault," Blake said, filling the awkward silence. He let her hand go and sat forward in his chair. "I screwed up. I didn't follow the rules of the training exercise. Actually, I pissed Dillon off."

"Dillon? The SWAT commander?"

"SWAT lead, yes. He slugged me, and I—"

"He hit you?" The agent sounded shocked.

Blake frowned. "It's no big deal. In his position, I'd have probably done the same thing. Haven't you ever punched someone?"

"Someone who was working for me? Never."

"Well, you're a better man than me. I've gotten in fights plenty of times."

"So I've heard. You had a bit of an anger management problem when you worked homicide out of Knoxville. Isn't that why you left? It was either quit or be fired? I believe there was concern over a grudge another officer had against you, maybe even a concern for your life if you stayed?"

Donna tensed. Could the agent be telling the truth? Was this why Blake had come to Destiny? Had the chief done him a favor, gotten him out before he could be fired? Or hurt? A light flush of red was creeping up his neck, which seemed answer enough.

"Reading someone's personnel files without a warrant is a crime," he said. "And I can't think of a single reason for a judge to give you one."

"I didn't have to read your files. All I had to do was make some calls to some friends on the force."

"I bet those friends enjoyed being woken up at, what, five or six in the morning, to spread gossip and innuendo that are entirely irrelevant to this case. Is that why it took you and your team so long to get here? You were wasting time digging into my past—for no good reason?"

Blake's voice hadn't risen during the exchange. Instead, it had grown steady, deeper than usual and deadly calm. She could practically feel the anger seeping out of his pores. And if she didn't know him as well as she did, she'd probably be scared right now. Then again, if he had these kinds of secrets he'd never shared, did she really know him at all?

Grant certainly didn't look impressed or

intimidated. He arched a brow as if amused. "That's the real reason your SWAT team lead punched you, isn't it? Because you couldn't control your anger and punched him first. Is that what happened?"

"No," Donna interrupted, starting to get just as agitated on Blake's behalf as he appeared to be. She'd deal with his secrets later, in private. But they were a team, and he deserved her loyalty in front of others—especially a stranger who came in supposedly to help them and was wasting their time with pettiness.

Both men had looked at her in surprise when she spoke, and they seemed to be waiting to see what else she wanted to say. She straightened her shoulders. "The truth is that Blake showed remarkable restraint when Dillon started accusing him of not being a team player. Blake had just captured two of three fake bad guys in the exercise, all by himself, and was proud of that. It caught him by surprise to realize that Dillon was furious over the whole thing. But Blake handled it well. Dillon's the one who didn't. Looking back, with the gift of hindsight, they both could have handled it a whole lot better. Both of them made mistakes. But the real mystery here is how any of this is helping us solve the case."

Blake, oblivious of the SSA watching, took

her hand again and squeezed. He nodded his thanks and let her hand go.

The agent frowned at both of them. He directed his next question to Blake. "Your lead was angry enough over your performance to punch you. Did he do anything else after that?"

Blake grew very still, his gaze locked on the agent. "Like what?"

"Like, I don't know, suspend you? Fire you?"

"Of course not," Donna intervened. "That would be overreacting. Dillon dismissed him, from the exercise. That's it."

His gaze slowly moved back to her. As she tried not to squirm beneath his scrutiny, she couldn't help thinking that Blake had been one hundred percent right up on the ridge when he'd argued about whether they should lie. He'd warned her that one lie would always lead to another and that things could get really complicated, really fast.

Things were definitely getting complicated.

She cleared her throat, which kept seeming to want to close up. "Again, I don't understand why you're wasting time questioning us. Everything you need to know about the case is in the reports that Blake and I spent the last few hours working up. We offered you free access to everything when you arrived. Even now your agents are out there reading those reports. All of this is in them."

Something akin to skepticism, maybe even disappointment, flashed across the agent's face as he folded his hands on top of the desk. "Since you both keep questioning my motives in asking these questions, I'll skip to the heart of the issue and be perfectly blunt. Does the name Jason Kent ring any bells?"

She sucked in a breath. Her stomach fluttered like a whole field of butterflies had just taken off inside.

"Jason Kent?" Blake asked. "Who's that?"

"The special agent I mentioned earlier," she said. "The one who was killed."

"Murdered, you mean," Grant snapped. "Because your team lead, Dillon Gray, along with your chief and your entire police force, misled Kent and gave him the runaround when he was here working on an embezzlement case. While you all tried to protect the woman that Dillon eventually married—"

"Of course we protected her. Ashley was innocent, and the FBI was trying to railroad her. Kent didn't give us a choice. The men behind the embezzlement, the people who were framing her, would have killed her if we'd let Kent lock her up."

"No need to review the details. I'm quite familiar with all the excuses given during the investigation that followed." He drew a deep breath before continuing. "That history between the Destiny Police Department and the bureau warns me to take everything anyone here tells me with a great deal of caution. I'm sure you've heard the mantra, trust but verify? That's what I'm doing here. Which means that I need to hear your alibis for where you were when Detective Carter was killed and the rest of the team disappeared. And I assure you my team will verify whatever stories you give me. So choose your words carefully."

Donna was too shocked and angry to speak. Thankfully Blake was the calm, measured one this time. He smoothly explained that after his altercation with Dillon, he left, and that Donna left her team shortly after because she was upset over what had happened. He detailed what had happened at the bar, and him trying to call Dillon and the team later on, before finally stopping at her house. The only time she had to jump in was to explain the time gap after she left the woods to when she found Blake at the bar. She'd been home, alone, showering, changing and trying to talk herself out of going after him. Which meant she might or might not have an alibi, depending on when Randy was killed.

"Well?" she asked, when she and Blake were

finished. "I'm assuming if you're asking for alibis that you've already read the autopsy report, even though neither of us has seen it yet. What was the time of death?"

"I prefer not to disclose that information until after we check out your claims—just in case you remember something else and change your stories."

Her mouth literally fell open. She couldn't believe he was acting this way. "You do realize that we can call Doc Brookes ourselves and ask him the T.O.D., don't you?"

"What I realize is that if you do, it could seriously jeopardize the investigation into your alibis. I strongly suggest that you not speak to anyone about the autopsy until you're cleared. If you're cleared."

She exchanged another stunned look with Blake. "Cleared? Really? We invited you here, thinking you could help us find the killer and bring back our team. But if you're going to waste your time going after us, consider yourself fired. You and your team can go back to Knoxville. We'll handle this on our own." She jumped up and headed toward the door.

"Donna," Blake called out. "Wait."

She stiffened, her hand on the doorknob. "Why? He's wasting our time."

"We invited him here to help us," Blake said.

"You and I don't have experience with kidnap-pings and ransom demands. Like it or not, we need to work together and park our hurt feel-ings at the door to get the job done." He waved toward the chair. "Please."

Grant clicked open the briefcase sitting on his desk. "Excellent points. But I'm afraid there's a lot more to it than that, Detectives. You've asked what took us so long to get here." He pulled some papers out of the briefcase and plopped them in front of him. "I think you'll both want to stick around and find out the answer to that question."

She turned and leaned back against the door, arms crossed. She refused to look at Blake. She didn't want to see the disappointment that was probably on his face. The professionalism she normally prided herself on had disintegrated long ago, probably around the twenty-hour mark of being up with no sleep.

Everything she was saying would probably come back to haunt her later. But at the moment, she just couldn't bring herself to care. She was too angry, too upset over Randy and the oth-ers, to bother with diplomacy at this point. And she wasn't sure they did need the help from the feds. The state police were happy to help them. And they'd worked kidnappings before. She was starting to understand why Chief Thornton disliked the FBI so much.

"Go ahead." She waved toward the papers in front of him. "Enlighten us. What took you close to seven hours to get here even though your field office is, what, forty-five minutes away? Go ahead. Explain. I'm all ears."

His brows rose. "Other than the fact that my immediate team and I were in the middle of the prosecution of an important, multi-year, multi-million-dollar case and had to wake a judge to postpone the trial so we could help save your teammates? Is that what you mean about delays? I'm sure you've heard of the Sanchez case."

Scorn dripped from his every word, and Donna couldn't help feeling chagrined. She *had* heard of the Sanchez case. Who hadn't? Sanchez was a reputed Colombian drug lord with a stranglehold over organized crime from Knoxville to Nashville. But she couldn't pull back on what she'd said now. She'd stepped in this with both feet. The only way out was to go forward. So she kept her mouth shut.

He shuffled through the papers as if searching for one in particular. Then he turned one facedown on top of the rest. "As I said before, due to our history, I was wary about working with the Destiny police. So I took some necessary protective precautions, just in case things didn't pass the smell test when I got here."

"What kind of precautions?" Blake asked.

Donna didn't ask. She'd glimpsed the letterhead on the paper he'd turned over. She already knew exactly what was coming. The only reason she didn't jump up right now and storm out was the off chance that she could be wrong.

She really, really hoped she was wrong.

"I'll answer that question with another. With your chief of police missing, who do you both report to?"

Blake looked at Donna, perhaps surprised she wasn't saying anything. "I imagine the mayor will have to appoint a temporary chief."

Grant nodded. "Correct. I stopped at his home on the way in to settle that issue." He flipped the paper over. "He was upset that no one had notified him about the murder and the kidnapping, or told him the FBI had been called in."

"Yes, well." Donna cleared her throat. "Honestly, I didn't even think about calling him. I'm sure I would have, sometime today, maybe after a nap to clear my head." She really was embarrassed that she hadn't notified the mayor. That should have been the first thing she did after returning to the station from the crime scene. But the chief was the one who always talked to the mayor. It hadn't even occurred to her.

"I'm sure you would have." Grant sounded as if he believed her on that score, at least. "But when we discussed who in the department should become the acting chief, imagine my surprise when he made me acting chief, even though Detective Waters was available and has nearly fifteen years on the force." He frowned. "By the way, the mayor's wife said to send you her regards. Is that significant for some reason?"

Any guilt she'd had over not being truthful with him evaporated. He obviously knew exactly what the significance was, or at least had to suspect the woman held a grudge against Donna. She was so angry right now, her whole body had tensed up. Her hands were balled into fists at her sides, and she was actually wondering what the penalties might be if she punched SSA Grant, and whether the satisfaction would be worth it.

"Good to know we've got you to take care of all the administrative stuff," Blake said hurriedly, as if to cut off anything she might say, or do. "That leaves us to do what we do best, investigate. Come on, Donna. Let's get back to work." He jumped up from his chair and motioned for her to go with him.

"Not so fast. Did I mention that the mayor was familiar with the training exercises you do up there on Hawkins Ridge? Apparently he had to approve the extra expense of paying three civilians to help in the exercise. He gave me their names and phone numbers so I could get their statements about what they saw up there. One of them lives one street over from the mayor. In the interest of getting as much information as I could, as quickly as possible, we stopped and spoke to him. Any guesses as to what the gentleman named Tim Nealy said really happened in the altercation with Dillon Gray? You know, as opposed to what you both told me?"

He pulled another piece of paper from the stack. It was a typed statement, with Tim's signature boldly scrawled across the bottom.

Donna's stomach seemed to drop to her feet as she glanced at Blake. He was standing stockstill, his face red, his mouth drawn into a tight line. But he wasn't looking at the agent. He was staring at her. Because of the lies she'd made him tell. It was collapsing all around them. And it was all her fault.

"SSA Grant," she said. "I can explain—"

"Explain what? That SWAT team leader and senior detective Dillon Gray fired Detective Sullivan, and yet hc's still here, pretending to be employed, working an active investigation? Or explain that you both lied about it to cover it up? Not exactly the ethical actions I'd expect of a police officer. Then again..." He waved his hands as if to encompass the entire station. "This is the Destiny Police Department. Color me *not* surprised."

She took a step toward the desk.

Blake grabbed her. "Don't. He's not worth it."

His gravelly voice had her looking at him in surprise. He was livid, but not at her. His anger was now directed at the agent.

"Go on." Grant motioned toward the door. "You're both fired. Hand over any remaining files or access codes my team needs. Then get out. I'll be generous and give you ten minutes. If you're still in the station after that, I'll have you both arrested."

Blake had to practically drag Donna out of the office. She couldn't seem to make her feet move. She was vacillating between anger and disbelief and horror that her actions were responsible for both her and Blake being dismissed, banned from the case. It was her worst nightmare come true—her friends were in trouble, but she had no way to help them.

Blake pulled the door shut behind them. "Breathe," he whispered in her ear. "You look like you're about to pass out."

"I can't believe that just happened. I've ruined everything. How are we going to save them now?"

"The same way we were going to save them

in the first place. With solid detective work. We're just going to have to do it without anyone else's help." He motioned to the big round clock on the wall above the front door. "We've got nine minutes left. We need to get as much information from his team as we can before our time is up. I say we hit up his leads for whatever intel they can share. They don't know we're off the case yet. They've got no reason not to be straight with us. I'll take the guys—Special Agents Joel Lawrence and Colin Lopez." He waved toward the first row of desks, where the two agents were both talking to another agent. "You take the woman—Special Agent Stacy Bell."

Stacy was sitting at a desk in the back row. She smiled at them, oblivious of the drama that had just happened with her boss.

Donna smiled back.

"Go." Blake gave her a little push toward Stacy as he headed toward Joel and Colin.

Donna was breathless by the time she and Blake hopped into his truck and shut the doors. She plopped a thin folder onto the bench seat between them, and Blake added two more folders to the stack, equally thin.

"You first," he said.

"I spoke to Officer Lynch before I left. He's

going to try to feed us information, keep us updated without letting anyone else know."

"Good thinking."

"I thought so. I also put my gloves in an evidence bag and slipped them to Lynch. I asked him if he could send them to a private lab to get DNA profiles on my dime, no questions asked. But that he needed to run those profiles against CODIS to see if we get a match on anyone's DNA in the system. If so, he's to call me immediately."

"Go, you," he said. "I forgot about the gloves. Hopefully it will pan out. What else?"

"Doc Brookes didn't conduct the autopsy. An M.E. from Maryville did, with Brookes assisting. That's fine and good. But other than to give a time of death—which is exactly when you and I were in the bar, thankfully, so we're in the clear there—the report is sketchy on details. I got a copy." She tapped the stack of folders. "I figure if we have questions, we can at least call Brookes. He won't care if we're fired or not. He'll see through that as bull. Cause of death is the obvious—gunshot. But get this. All of the samples taken during the autopsy were sent to the FBI lab, not our state lab. Seems to me that will take way more time and could delay the investigation."

"Agreed. That's odd. Did Stacy say why they did that?"

"Grant's orders, something about needing to cross every *t* and dot every *i* for this one because officers are the victims in this case."

"It's also a kidnapping case, with speed more important than anything else." Blake shook his head. "I don't get it."

"Me either. I have a copy of the crime scene report, too. It was pretty thorough. They found footprints that seemed inconsistent with the kinds of boots our team wears. And a ton of fingerprints in the barn. It'll take a while to see whether any of those prints belong to a viable suspect, though. They took blood samples from the body and inside the barn. But, again, instead of sending them to our lab, they're on their way to Quantico. Yet another delay. What did the guys tell you?"

"They were concerned about notifying the families of the deceased and the kidnap victims. I told them the contact information is all in that spreadsheet you put together, but that we'd already notified Randy's mom. They appreciated that. I didn't tell them that the wives were on a cruise."

She blinked in surprise. "You withheld information?"

"Yeah, well. Once you start down the path…"

He shrugged. "I was going to tell them, but one of the other agents came up to ask a question, a really simple question. And it got me talking to Colin Lopez about the team that came in with him. He admitted that other than him, Special Agent Joel Lawrence and SA Stacy Bell, the others are pretty green, without a lot of experience. He said, normally, on a case like this, he would have expected more senior agents to be brought along. But they were all stretched pretty thin by this Sanchez thing. Even with a court delay, a lot of them were told to remain in Knoxville to try to gather more evidence to strengthen the case. Even though the case is supposed to be locked up tight. Seems strange to me."

"So, let me get this straight," she said. "The top investigator thinks our kidnapping is so important that he postpones a major case to lend us his expertise. He brings his top three leads, who were all working the Sanchez case before this. But then he chooses green new recruits for the rest of his team? We got the A team at the top and the D team at the bottom. That doesn't make sense."

"I agree. Without saying it that way, I did hint around about Grant being uptight. One of the agents, Lawrence, laughed and said they'd all noticed the same thing and were walking on eggshells around him this morning. Normally, he's supposedly this polite, nice guy, who's super family-oriented and a great person to work with. For the past few weeks, he's been a real bear. None of them seemed to understand why."

"Did you ask if it was the pressure of the Sanchez case?" she asked.

"I did. But they said the case has been going on for years. There hasn't been anything recently that would explain it. His wife and kids headed off on vacation last week—without him. They figure that might be it. That maybe he and his wife had a fight or something and she left him. He hasn't said one word about his family since."

She nodded. "Trouble at home could explain a lot, not that I want to give the jerk an excuse for how he's acting. So what do we do now? We have to get some sleep. Willpower alone isn't going to keep my eyes open. But I hate the thought of not doing something to keep the investigation moving forward. Trusting Grant to take care of it doesn't sit well with me. But what bothers me more than anything is the idea of him notifying Ashley and the others about what has happened. I sure wish we could talk to them before any feds do."

"Maybe we can. When does the ship dock again?"

"Today, about five o'clock, in Miami. The

feds have a field office there. I guarantee they'll send some agents to interview them. All I know to do is try to call Ashley once they dock and hope I reach her before the feds. I hate telling her news like that over the phone, though."

"I agree. And I want to interview all of them, anyway, to augment your timeline and look for any evidence that any of this is personal—that maybe one member of the SWAT team, or even the chief, was targeted. That's hard to do over the phone."

She lifted her hands in a helpless gesture. "I don't see what choice we have."

He tapped the steering wheel, as if deep in thought. "Too bad we don't have access to a private plane. We could skip security, avoid the wait for a scheduled flight and go straight to Miami without any stops in between. We could sleep on the way and make it to the port long before the agents felt they needed to be at the dock, giving us a chance to, I don't know, get in position somewhere and somehow intercept the wives before the agents locate them."

He shook his head again. "I don't even know how we'd manage that, even if we did have access to a private plane. I don't know anyone with enough money to own one, let alone have a pilot available to fly it even if they'd agree to take us."

"I do."

He frowned. "What are you talking about?"

"The Carroll family. Remember, we saved their daughter from drowning last summer? They were tourists, taking the scenic route home to Nashville, passing through Maryville after vacationing in the Smoky Mountains. Remember?"

He slowly nodded. "Yeah, yeah, I do. We were investigating a robbery, and it led us to a hotel in Maryville. We were walking by the pool, and their little girl had somehow gotten out of their hotel room and jumped in the water. She couldn't swim, and you saved her life."

"Well, we both saved her is how I remember it. I dragged her out, and you gave her CPR. Regardless, the father is a commercial pilot, and the mom is one of those society ladies, comes from money. They have private planes in airports all over Tennessee. And they flat-out told us if we ever needed anything to give them a call. I can't personally think of anything I've needed more right this minute."

"Me either. And the worst they can do is say no. Let's do it."

Chapter Ten

Donna glared at the two FBI agents waiting at the other end of the terminal, right where the cruise ship passengers were about to disembark.

"So much for our grand plan to beat the feds here. This place is locked up tighter than an airport, and those two agents have the security team's ear."

With their dark suits and black ties, they were hard to miss. Especially since one of them was holding up a sign with Destiny, Tennessee, written on it, and the other had a sign with the last names of the SWAT team members' wives. Security was letting them stand right at the gangplank exit, several yards ahead of everyone else who was waiting for their loved ones.

"Did you try Ashley's phone again?" Blake asked.

"Are you kidding? I've texted and called her and the others more than when I was searching for you the day of that stupid paintball exercise. They must have all turned their phones off, unplugged from the world, while they enjoyed their cruise. There's no way we'll be able to get their attention first. Everyone from their ship will come down that same walkway, like hamsters through a tunnel. And we can't exactly shove our way in front of the agents."

Blake turned in a slow circle, looking around. "Maybe we don't have to. I've got an idea."

Donna glanced over her shoulder. Other than the restrooms, all she saw was a busy ticket counter, probably checking in passengers for the cruise ship that shared this terminal. The electronic board above the counter showed that the other ship was due to leave for a seven-day cruise to the Bahamas in a little over an hour.

"What's your idea?" she asked. "Pull the fire alarm?"

He winked. "That would be highly illegal, not to mention dangerous for anyone in the terminal. I prefer a more subtle approach. Keep an eye on the walkway. Call me know when you see our party."

She was so surprised by that playful wink that she stood frozen in place as he walked toward the ticket counter. He looked back and motioned toward the gangplank, reminding her she had a job to do. Clearing her throat, she nodded and turned back to watch for Ashley and the others.

A full minute passed, and she was about to turn around again to check on him, when the noise level inside the terminal changed. Passengers from the ship that she and Blake were waiting for were visible in the distance now, colorful shirts and Bermuda shorts filling the tunnel as the crowd hurried through.

Donna edged around several people in the crowd, craning her neck to see. A puff of white hair caught her attention. She squinted, trying to bring the woman into focus, and couldn't help wondering if a trip to the eye doctor was in her future. She'd been squinting a lot lately. A few seconds later, the woman's face came into focus—Claire Thornton, the chief's wife. To her right, Ashley Gray was pushing a baby stroller. To her left, Chris's and Max's wives— Julie and Bex—were smiling and gesturing with their hands as they spoke animatedly about something.

A quick glance at the two FBI agents revealed they were still standing the same as before, looking bored as they held up their signs. They must not have spotted the women yet among the crowd. But it wouldn't be long now—assuming they knew what the wives looked like. Maybe they didn't, and were relying completely on the signs? The problem, of course, was that it really didn't matter. As soon as the wives saw the signs, they'd stop and ask what was going on.

She and Blake really should have come up with a better plan. Or, at least, a plan at all. They'd been so certain when they arrived that they'd be able to get past security and onto the top of the gangplank to intercept their friends. But that hadn't happened. Even flashing their badges—which they'd snuck out with them after being fired—hadn't bought them any extra consideration from the security staff. They were told to wait with the families, something about causing a dangerous situation on the small gangplank if they tried to intercept someone there. Supposedly waiting out here was safer and would accomplish the same goal.

So what were they supposed to do now?

She whirled around looking for Blake. His height made him easy to see above the crowd. He was grinning and passing something to a buxom blonde behind the ticket counter. The light flush on her cheeks and the flirty smile had Donna's hands coiling into fists. She was about to whirl around in disgust—and more than a little jealousy—when the woman picked up a desk phone and punched some buttons. The intercom speakers crackled overhead.

"Attention, there's been a change in terminals

for the packages from Destiny, Tennessee. Packages are arriving now at Terminal D. Repeat, packages from Destiny, Tennessee, are arriving now at Terminal D. Thank you."

Packages? Terminal D? That terminal was on the opposite side of the concourse. Blake caught her gaze and gave her a thumbs-up sign, a big Cheshire Cat grin curving his lips as he started toward her. Was that his big plan? Flirt with the ticket agent to make her announce that silly message that wouldn't fool anyone? Blake motioned toward something behind her.

She spun around just in time to see the two FBI agents sprinting past her, a panicked look on their faces as they raced down the concourse—*away* from Ashley and the other wives, who had just stopped beside the security guards, perplexed looks on their faces. They'd probably seen the signs the agents were holding and heard the bizarre announcement over the intercom. It had worked. Blake's crazy, ridiculous plan had worked.

"Come on." His voice was suddenly by her ear. "Let's grab our friends before the agents realize what happened."

"I can't believe they fell for that. It was…brilliant," she admitted as they hurried forward.

"Cost me twenty bucks and a dinner date. Too bad I won't be here when she gets off her shift. She seemed like a nice woman. I hated lying to her."

Donna's hands were curling into fists again. "I'm sure she'll survive the disappointment."

"Donna, what are you doing here?" It was Bex who made that exclamation as she and the others rushed past the security guards to meet them. True to form for law-enforcement families, it was alarm, rather than pleasure, in Bex's and the others' expressions.

"Well?" Ashley said from beside Bex, her brow furrowing with concern as she glanced from Blake to Donna. "What's going on? And what was that announcement over the intercom about packages from Destiny? Is Dillon okay?"

"What about Chris?" Julie insisted, her face pale with worry.

"Ladies, we'll answer all your questions in a few minutes," Blake said while Donna was still struggling to speak past the sudden lump in her throat. "First, there's a security issue that has us concerned for your safety. We need to get out of here. Now."

Again, their experience as the wives of police officers kicked in. Even though they all looked worried, they didn't hesitate. They moved as one toward the exit, where Blake was directing them. Donna took up the lead, heading toward the nearest doors, while Blake moved beside

Bex and took the handle of one of the two suit-cases she'd been pulling along. Next to her, like a mother hen, Claire Thornton was shooing ev-eryone forward, having picked up on the ur-gency in Blake's voice.

"Do you have any other bags to get?" Donna asked.

Ashley shook her head. "Bex has mine, or did." She nodded her thanks to Blake, her hands on the stroller with her little daughter inside, thankfully sleeping through everything.

The doors whooshed open, and the group of six adults and a stroller headed outside as one.

"Where to?" Claire asked, sounding like a drill sergeant.

"Over there." Blake motioned toward a spot at the curb. Then he waved his hand in the air.

Similar to the airport, no one was allowed to idle in a vehicle out front. Security guards pa-trolled up and down the now-crowded walkway to enforce that rule. But the limo Donna and Blake had hired was already zipping out of the parking lot across from the terminal and weav-ing around a line of cabs, ignoring their honk-ing horns. A moment later, the limo screeched to a halt in front of them, and the trunk popped open.

Blake and the driver met at the trunk and began stashing the women's luggage inside.

"Wait," Ashley said. "The car seat for Letha, it's in my suitcase."

"There's a car seat in the back of the limo for her," Donna said.

Ashley gave her a grateful look and lifted her sleeping daughter out of the stroller. While everyone was piling into the car, Donna glanced around. The two agents who'd taken Blake's bait and had run toward the other terminal burst out of the building, chests heaving with exertion as they scanned the crowds.

"Hurry," Donna urged. "Everyone get in."

Blake looked past her, his jaw tightening. "I've got this one," he told the driver, and grabbed the last suitcase.

The driver hurried to get into the car and started the engine. Blake slammed the trunk and he and Donna hopped in with the others.

"Go, go, go," Blake said.

The agents were rushing toward them, looking around, as if they hadn't spotted them yet.

The limo sped away from the curb.

"Slow down," Blake cautioned. "We don't want to attract any attention."

The driver nodded and slowed.

Donna watched the agents stop at the curb where they'd just been, still looking around.

"They didn't see us," she said.

"It won't take them long to figure it out," Blake warned. "How far to the next car?"

"It's on the other side of the terminal. Two minutes away in this traffic." The driver weaved around a slow-moving cab.

"Would someone please tell us what's going on?" Ashley demanded, her voice firm but quiet so as not to wake her daughter. "Who is it? Who's hurt? Or…just tell us who it is. Please."

"Let's focus on getting away from the port first," Blake said. "When we reach the plane, we'll explain everything."

"You'll explain everything right now, Detective Sullivan," Claire ordered, sounding just like the chief. "You're worrying these ladies and me. We have a right to know what's going on."

"It's Max, isn't it?" Bex's face was drawn as she lowered her cell phone. "I just tried to call him. He's not answering."

"Neither is Chris." Julie exchanged a nervous glance with Bex and turned her phone around toward Donna. "I just turned this one on, and you've called me ten times today. Come on, Donna. What happened? Has there been an accident? What?"

The limo turned the corner and swerved into a parking lot beside another limo, this one white instead of black.

"As far as we know, your husbands are fine,"

Donna said, when Blake seemed to be struggling for words. "But we believe you're in danger. Please. Let's switch to the other car before we answer your questions. You're being followed."

"Those agents in the terminal?" Ashley asked. "They had to be feds. FBI maybe? They stuck out like a sore thumb. But before we reached them, they took off."

Donna nodded as the car stopped and both the driver and Blake hopped out. "Yes."

"Why are we running from FBI agents?" Ashley demanded. "And don't tell me to shut up and get in the other car. I'm not going anywhere until you give us something. The driver is moving the luggage to the other limo now, in case you were worried about him overhearing. Out with it, Donna. What's going on?"

She realized they had a mutiny on their hands if she didn't tell them. She cleared her throat and gave them all an apologetic look. "I wanted to break this to you more gently, but there's no easy way to tell you. Yesterday, Randy Carter was murdered."

A collective gasp went up from the women. Ashley's hand was suddenly grasping Donna's. "I'm so sorry. I know you and Randy were especially close. Was it in the line of duty?"

"Yes." Her voice cracked. "Yes, it was. I'm sure he was very brave."

Ashley's brow furrowed, and she exchanged a puzzled look with Bex. "You're *sure*? It sounds like you're guessing. You weren't there?"

She shook her head.

As if sensing her mother's tension, Ashley's little girl began to cry in the car seat next to her. But rather than comfort her as she would normally do, Ashley stared intently at Donna.

"Then what happened?" Her voice shook with a mixture of anger and fear. "We went dark on the cruise—no phones, no social media, no internet. It was all part of unplugging, relaxing, really getting away from the world. But now you've got me borderline terrified, because ever since we docked and turned our phones back on, none of us have been able to reach our families. And you just told us that Randy has been killed. And apparently we're on the run from the FBI. For God's sake, Donna. Tell us what's going on. Please, please tell us that Dillon and the others are okay."

The pleading look in her friend's eyes ripped another piece from Donna's heart, adding a new fissure on top of the gaping hole that Randy's death had created. She took both of Ashley's hands in hers, and Ashley held on to her like a lifeline, her whole body shaking as she waited for Donna to destroy her world.

"Try not to panic. Blake and I believe they're okay. There's still hope. But Dillon, Max, Chris, even the chief, they've all been kidnapped."

Chapter Eleven

It wasn't the type of hotel that Blake would have chosen for the next phase in their plan. One, because he couldn't afford it. And two, he wouldn't have chosen to stop at a hotel at all. The private plane was waiting to take all of them back to McGhee Tyson Airport, just down the road from Destiny, and he was anxious to continue the investigation. But Chris's wife, Julie, had plenty of money, courtesy of a wealthy grandmother, and had insisted on getting them a large suite in a five-star hotel to regroup and discuss what was going on. And the other wives had pretty much refused to get on a plane until they'd heard everything Blake and Donna could tell them about their husbands.

He sat beside Donna on one of the couches, his arm around her shoulders, offering his support. Right now he didn't care one whit what the others might think. What mattered was that Donna had looked so bleak and fragile as she began to recite the tale about finding Randy and the note. And when he'd tentatively put his arm around her, instead of pulling away, she settled into the curve of his body and gave him a smile of gratitude.

"That's it," Donna said, spreading her hands out in a helpless gesture. "We really don't know much at this point. But the fact that whoever kidnapped them left a ransom note is encouraging. It gives us hope that they're still okay."

"I'll pay it," Julie said. "Whatever the amount. How much are they asking? I can write a check right now."

Donna gave Blake a worried glance.

He gently massaged her shoulder and answered Julie's question. "Rodney Lynch, one of the uniformed officers back in Destiny, agreed to give us updates and said he'd call as soon as a ransom demand was made. But so far, there's been no contact from the kidnappers."

The four women exchanged worried glances, before Ashley once again took the lead as if they'd secretly nominated her as their spokesperson. "It's what, seven o'clock now? That means over twenty-four hours have passed since they…since they killed Randy and left the note. Is that normal for kidnappers to wait that long before stating their terms?"

"Honestly," Blake said, "I don't know. I've

never worked a kidnapping case before. But the FBI certainly has. I'm sure they're doing everything they can to resolve this without anyone else getting hurt."

Ashley rolled her eyes. "Spare me the faith in the FBI speech. I was almost railroaded into prison by them. And they can't have brought their top team down here if their poor decision-making skills meant cutting you two out of the investigation. That's the most idiotic thing I've heard so far. You're the locals. You know everything about Destiny and the surrounding area. It makes sense that you should be in the thick of this, evaluating the evidence. Not sitting on the sidelines."

"Well," Donna said, "to be fair, we did try to cover up that Blake was fired. It's understandable that the SSA thought he needed to cut us loose. I can't imagine what would happen if he found out about us touching the note."

"Thank goodness you did, or we might not even know the others had been kidnapped. At least this way, we can hope, as you said before," Ashley said. "So what can we do to help? What do you want from us?"

"Victimology," Blake said. "It's when you study the victims to find out—"

"Everything you can about them to build a timeline and try to identify suspects who might have targeted them," Ashley finished. "We're cops' wives. We know all about how investigations work. I'm sure all of us will be happy to fill in any gaps in your timeline and tell you anything you want to know. Right, ladies?"

A collective murmur of agreement went up from the group. A cry sounded from the bedroom. Ashley started to get up, but Claire waved her back down.

"I'll check on her," she said. "You all keep talking. From the sounds of that note and everything else, I don't think anyone targeted my Bill. They were after the team. The only reason Bill was on that exercise at all was that…" She gave Blake an apologetic look. "Sorry, sweetie. Cops do talk to their wives, and I've heard there have been some…issues with you and how you haven't been gelling with the team. Dillon asked him to be there. I think he expected something might happen—with you, not the rest of this."

"No apology necessary," Blake said to her. "Thank you for being candid."

She gave him a sad smile and headed into the bedroom.

Nearly an hour later, Donna set her notes on the end table by the couch and sat back. "I don't get it. The timelines are complete. Every gap is filled in. And yet we don't have one single new clue about who could be behind this."

"Sure we do," Blake said. "The person behind this isn't interested in anyone on the SWAT team, or the chief, as Claire said." He nodded to her. She nodded back from the chair where she was rocking the baby.

"What, then?" Ashley asked. "Was it about Randy? And the rest of them just…" She swallowed hard. "The rest of them got caught up in it, and the ransom note is a diversion? The bad guys want to get out of town while the police are waiting for a ransom phone call?" Her last word was a broken whisper that barely made it past her lips before she burst into tears.

Donna gave Blake a look of pure misery before joining Bex and Julie in an effort to comfort Ashley. Many tears were shed before they all seemed to gather themselves.

Bex rubbed Ashley's back and put her arm around her waist. "Is there anything else you needed from us? I think we're all ready to head back home now." She frowned. "Or, I guess we should contact the local FBI? Since they wanted to talk to us? I know you two wanted to talk to us first because, otherwise, you wouldn't have been able to get your timeline information. But since the FBI is actively working the case, seems to me we should go ahead and make contact instead of hiding."

"I agree," Blake said. "That's probably better than just hopping on the plane with Donna and me. There's no point in not talking to them now. I can't thank you enough for speaking to us, though. You never know what will matter in a case, what little piece of information might eventually make all the puzzle pieces fit together. I just wish we could have resolved all of this before you came back from your law-enforcement family cruise."

Bex snorted. "Law-enforcement family cruise? That's a joke if I ever heard one. I don't know what happened. Some kind of mix-up, I guess. That cruise was a singles cruise. We were the only married ones on board. And there weren't any other police family members that I saw. Let me just say, we didn't exactly fit in."

Blake frowned. "You were the only law-enforcement family members on the whole ship? Are you sure?"

"Well, as sure as we can be," Bex said. "When there weren't any police-themed dinners or announcements or anything, we thought it was odd, and we started asking around. None of the staff seemed to have a clue what we were talking about when we mentioned the charity that funded our cruise." She glanced back and forth between Donna and Blake. "Why? Is that significant?"

Blake shook his head. "Probably not. Mix-ups

like that happen all the time. Still, I'll note it and follow up, just to make sure it's not related. What was the name of the charity?"

Bex looked to Julie for help. "Do you remember the name? It was something really simple like *Fun for Families*. Was that it?"

Julie was nodding as she pulled a business card out of her purse and handed it to Blake. "It was completely arranged from beginning to end, all prepaid. Even if they ended up accidentally putting us on the wrong boat from the rest of the law-enforcement families, as far as I'm concerned, the cruise was great. We really had a good time." Her bottom lip trembled, but she drew a deep breath and held it together.

"We're all exhausted," Ashley said, once again speaking for the group. "I think we should freshen up, check out and head to the FBI field office to answer their questions. You two don't have to wait your plane on us. We've got commercial airline tickets already. We'll just switch to a morning flight so we have time to talk to the feds today."

Blake left Donna to help them make arrangements for the FBI to pick them up at the hotel while he headed into the kitchenette, where it was more quiet. He made a call to one of his contacts back in Knoxville to get more information on the charity. By the time he finished the call, his stomach was churning, and his blood running cold. He rushed into the main part of the suite.

"What time are the feds getting here?"

Donna rose from the couch. "What's wrong?"

"What time?"

She checked her watch. "About thirty minutes. Why? What are you—"

"Grab your things. We have to get out of here. Now."

"Blake—"

"No time, Donna. We have to get out of here before the feds get here. Trust me on this." He made a quick call to the limo driver, telling him to bring the car around, while the others grabbed their things, and Ashley put the baby in the stroller.

Blake could say one thing about these ladies. They were as well trained as their husbands. He didn't know anyone else who could have gotten things together and been in the limo, being whisked away from the hotel, in under six minutes.

"Okay, yet again, we're running from the very men who are trying to find our husbands," Ashley complained as she patted her daughter in the car seat beside her, trying to keep her whimpering from turning into a full-fledged tantrum. "Why?"

"A friend of mine did a quick trace on that charity," Blake said. "It was set up as a one-time thing and traced back to a shell company—basically a fake company like criminals use to cover their tracks. If they were a true charity, there wouldn't be any problem tracing it back. Because the supposed donors would want to be able to claim their contributions on their taxes. My friend also said that they'd been looking into the charity because one of the wives in Knoxville complained that the charity never announced the winners of the cruise tickets. It's as if the charity was set up for one purpose—to give just you ladies tickets. I called the cruise line, too. They didn't know anything at all about the charity or a law-enforcement family cruise on any of their ships."

Donna stared at him. "So a fake charity just happens to send the wives of our now missing officers out of town for a week. And no one else? Quite the coincidence, which means no way is it a coincidence. Why would they do that? What do they stand to gain? And what does this have to do with the FBI?"

"As to why and what they gain, I have no idea. But regarding the FBI, I have one name for you—Lopez."

"Lopez. As in SSA Grant's assistant, Lopez?"

"One and the same. The city balked at issuing a permit for the charity event. Guess who intervened and basically sweet-talked the city into granting the permit?"

"Lopez." Donna's brow furrowed in confusion. "But the FBI has no authority over something like that, unless…unless it has to do with white-collar crime or cyber-crime. Maybe they were investigating the charity and needed the event to move forward to help them gather more evidence? That could explain Lopez's involvement."

"Excuse me." This time it was Julie who had a question. "Who are Grant and Lopez?"

"They're both part of the FBI team in Destiny investigating Randy's murder and your husbands' kidnappings. Supervisory Special Agent Richard Grant is in charge. Colin Lopez, Stacy Bell and Joel Lawrence are his leads, basically his assistants, his right-hand, top investigators. All four of them were handling a high-profile case—the Sanchez drug kingpin case—before getting the judge to grant a delay so they could help in Destiny. Apparently they're supposed to be top guys from the Knoxville field office, and the bureau thought they were their best chance at getting the Destiny case resolved as quickly and safely as possible. There are some other FBI guys they brought with them, too. But Lopez is one of the top dogs."

"Okay, so you think, what, he's dirty? This Lopez guy? Just because his name comes up in support of the charity and he's working the Destiny case?" Julie continued.

"If it was just those two things, I probably wouldn't. But his boss, Grant, seemed way over the top to me in how he went after the two of us—almost as if that was his goal from the start. Each thing by itself seems okay, has a perfectly reasonable explanation. But, together, it starts to pile up and look suspicious."

"Each thing. Is there more you haven't told us?"

The suspicions swirling through his mind had made perfect sense back in the hotel, with the FBI on the way. But now he wasn't so sure. Saying it out loud would just emphasize how little they knew and would make his doubts seem even more far-fetched.

"It's an ongoing investigation," Donna said. "We can't go into everything right now. Just suffice it to say, at this point, there are too many questions around Grant, Lopez and potentially others for us to feel comfortable with you being around them. We can pass the timeline information from you to Grant through one of the Destiny officers. That way, if our fears prove to be wrong, no harm done to their investigation. And if you can all lie low somewhere for a few days, or until we find the team, that would take a huge weight of worry off Blake's and my shoulders, knowing for sure that you're safe. Is that something you would consider doing?"

Julie looked at the others. One by one, they each nodded their agreement. She turned back to Blake and Donna. "Okay. We'll do it. But only if you follow through on the timeline data, like you said. I know I'd never forgive myself if something happened to Chris because I didn't speak to the FBI over a hunch that ended up proving false. I want them to have that information. And I don't see being able to stay away more than a couple of days, tops. I want to be out there, searching for Chris and the others, not holed up in a hotel room wringing my hands."

Alarmed, Blake said, "Please don't do that. Until we know the goal behind the kidnapping, I implore you to stay off the radar. Maybe you can hire some personal security guys for the duration, too. Couldn't hurt. I know my mind would be more at ease if you did."

Julie nodded. "I think that's a great idea. I'll take care of that. We'll stay gone as long as we can, but if it's more than a few days, I can't promise you won't see every one of us back in Destiny, demanding an update from the FBI. Put yourself in our place, Blake. If Donna was missing, I suspect you'd move heaven and earth to be involved in the case and find her."

He blinked, not sure what to say to that. But Julie was already huddling with the others, speaking in low tones as they discussed something. He chanced a quick look at Donna. She was staring at him, her brow furrowed as if she was thinking about Julie's statement. He swallowed and looked away. Was he that transparent? Were his feelings for her out for everyone to see? Or had Julie just assumed he'd be that invested in trying to protect her because they were partners?

"All right." Julie turned back around. "We've agreed on a location, where we're going to stay for now. We'll—"

"No." Blake held up a hand to stop her. "It's better if we don't know the details. That way, if we end up being interviewed by Grant or the others, we can honestly tell them that we don't know where you are. The limo driver can drop Donna and me off at a car rental place. We'll get to the airport on our own from there. I wouldn't want you ladies with us, again, in case the FBI is watching the airport. I imagine they'll be watching the terminal for your commercial flight you scheduled, waiting for you to show up. So you'll need to drive wherever you go. They don't know about Donna and me taking the private plane, or even that we're here. So we should be able to catch our flight with none the wiser."

"Okay. Anything else we should know?" Ashley spoke up this time, glancing from him to Donna and back again.

"Burner phones," Donna suggested.

"Right. Good idea," Blake said. "You can stop at one of those postal stores in a strip mall and mail your personal phones back home. They can be traced, so keeping them with you isn't a good idea, just in case someone really is going to try to find you. Make one stop, and one stop only, at a bank and draw out enough cash to get you by for at least a week. Purchase a prepaid phone without a plan of any kind to keep your name out of it. That's what Donna means by a burner phone—something that can't be traced back to you. After that, don't go to the bank or an ATM and don't use any of your credit cards anywhere. You need to go all cash and leave no electronic trace."

Ashley frowned at him. "We'll need a credit card to rent a hotel room."

"A five-star hotel, sure. But if you keep a low profile, you should be able to pay a cash deposit up front to convince someone to rent to you. I'm not saying you need to stay in a dive. Just pick a clean, modern hotel off one of the interstate exits, and you should be okay."

None of them looked happy with his plan, but to give them credit, they didn't argue. Half an hour later, Blake was driving with Donna to the airport in a fairly generic four-door sedan, after watching the wives head in the opposite direction, down the highway, in the limo.

"I hope we did the right thing back there," Donna said.

"Me, too. You know there's more to this than what I told them, don't you?" He steered around a slow-moving car, before moving back into the right lane.

She nodded. "I'm starting to feel that way, yes. Nothing about how the case is being handled feels right. The way the evidence was delayed by being sent to the FBI lab instead of a local one that's more than capable of processing everything, that alone raises questions in my mind. Added with everything else, the doubts are definitely piling up. Something is way off here."

"Remember what Ashley said earlier, asking whether the ransom note was just a diversion? No one has made contact with details about how to pay. That really struck me. Not that it was a diversion as much as a delay tactic. It puts things on hold while we wait to hear from the kidnappers. And that's not the only delay that has come up."

"You're talking about the Sanchez trial," she said. "Which was literally delayed because the main FBI guys were needed for our Destiny investigation?"

"Yes. I wouldn't think much of it, except that Officer Lynch updated us on the way here saying there wasn't any progress that he could tell with the investigation. Kind of surprising if the FBI's best guys out of the Knoxville field office were diverted specifically because they're so good. Wouldn't you expect more from them?"

Again, he passed a few cars before moving back to the right. A sign up ahead showed they were just a couple of exits from the airport. Blake had already called ahead to notify the pilot to be ready.

She nodded slowly. "I would expect more from the FBI, normally. You're right. Time is supposedly of the essence in a kidnapping situation. But instead of being proactive and pounding the pavement, trying to find our guys, it would seem that they're sitting back, waiting for first contact—or second, if you count the note. And like Ashley said earlier, it doesn't make sense to remove you and me from the case if the main goal is to find the missing cops. Who better to help navigate the local scene than the only two remaining detectives, two detectives who could have given them a lot more information about their missing peers to help them zero in on potential grudges, suspects who might have an ax to grind against Dillon and the others?"

Blake shook his head. "The more I think about it, the more all of this seems horribly wrong. If we assume our FBI guys are dirty, then what's the motive? Why kill Randy? Why kidnap the others?"

"Maybe the kidnappers know that Chris's wife is wealthy," Donna said. "Maybe that's why the note talks about a ransom—because they know Julie can pay."

"Except that no one has given instructions for how to deliver the money. The note didn't even list a specific amount so the families could gather the funds. The longer we go without a specific demand, the thinner the idea of kidnapping for ransom seems."

"Then why kidnap our team?" she asked.

He tapped his hands on the steering wheel as he reasoned it out. "Okay, how about this. What's the one consistent thread that keeps coming up as we talk this through?"

"Delays. No question," she said.

He nodded. "What if the delay in the Sanchez trial is the only delay that matters? What if everything else is secondary, and all of this is intended to divert the FBI's attention to Destiny and put a stop to the criminal case?"

She shook her head. "That doesn't make sense, though, does it? From what I've heard on the news channels, the Sanchez case is wrapped up tight. A delay won't change the outcome. Sanchez's empire is about to come crashing down around him. He's going to go to prison for the rest of his life."

He put his blinker on for the airport exit. "Look at it from another angle. Our FBI guys went from high-profile case to high-profile case. Kidnapping an entire SWAT team is a big deal. And yet, they've managed to keep it out of the news so far. So it seems unlikely that the person behind this cares about media attention. If they did, they'd have leaked information and it would have already hit all the major networks."

"Okay," she said. "I'm with you so far."

"All the kidnapping has accomplished at this point is that it diverted resources and put the law-enforcement community's attention on Destiny instead of Knoxville."

Blake steered the car down the exit ramp and followed the signs to the car rental company's parking lot.

"All right." Donna picked up the line of reasoning. "We have kidnappers who don't seem to be in a hurry to get any money. And we have a case that diverted resources from another case. No matter how we look at this, it circles back to the FBI and the Sanchez case. Assuming that Sanchez's goons are responsible for Randy's death and the kidnappings—which seems like a logical leap—we need to figure out how this helps Sanchez."

Blake parked the car. "As soon as we land at McGhee Tyson Airport, I think we should head to where all of this—whatever this is—seems to have started."

She nodded. "We're going to Knoxville."

Chapter Twelve

Even though they'd both dozed on the plane to and from Miami, it hadn't been what Donna thought of as "quality" sleep. She was so exhausted, she fell asleep the moment she leaned back in the passenger seat of the little blue Ford Focus they rented at the McGhee Tyson Airport. And she didn't wake up until Blake shook her awake in a hotel parking lot somewhere in Knoxville.

She rubbed her bleary eyes, a flush of guilt heating her face when she saw how tired he looked. "I'm sorry. I know you're just as wiped out as I am. I should have offered to drive."

He gave her a sleepy, incredibly sexy grin. "We'd have been in a ditch just a few blocks down the road from the airport when you fell into a coma. You sure do fall asleep fast."

He leaned over the back of the seat and grabbed their satchels that contained just a few days' worth of clothes and toiletries—plus their pistols and ammo, of course.

"Where are we?" she asked.

"The neon lights spelling out *Embassy Suites* doesn't give it away?"

"Ha ha."

He smiled again. She noticed he smiled more when he was tired, as if it was the only time he ever truly let his guard down. It did incredible things to his already handsome face, making her stomach tighten with want.

If she wasn't so tired, she might have jumped him just to finally get that crazy desire out of her system—and find out once and for all if he wanted her, too. But as tired as they both were, she knew that wasn't even on the radar.

As they walked under the portico to the front doors, she asked, "Seriously. Where are we?"

"Knoxville West, just off I-40. I've been here before, so I knew it was decent and clean. I called on the way and made a reservation. They only had a few rooms left. Since I couldn't get two on the same floor, I settled for a suite. Hope that's okay. It's got a separate bedroom and a sectional couch with a pullout sofa bed."

"I wouldn't care if we had to share the same bed at this point. I could probably sleep on the floor in the lobby right now."

His eyes had widened when she mentioned

sharing a bed, but he recovered quickly, with another one of those sexy grins. "I think they frown on people camping in the lobby here. Let's at least get up to the room before you sink into your coma again."

She couldn't help wondering why he'd been to this hotel before. He'd lived in Knoxville, so why would he stay in a hotel instead of his house? Or apartment? Or wherever he lived? Had he brought a date here rather than take her back to his place? And why did that thought make her feel so pathetically jealous? It wasn't like they'd ever dated. And even though she'd been mooning after him for months, he'd always been the perfect gentleman—much to her dismay.

"Earth to Donna. You in there somewhere?" He was waving his hand in front of her face.

She blinked and realized they were standing in front of an open elevator, and he was holding the door for her. "Sorry," she mumbled as she stepped inside.

When the door shut, and he pressed the button for the fourth floor, she realized she'd zombied out at the registration desk and hadn't even remembered him getting the room keys.

"We'll have to keep up with our expenses so I can pay you my half," she said. "You've been buying everything. Heck, I should pay *all* of our expenses. You need to conserve your funds in case this doesn't end the way I hope it will and you don't get your job back."

"No worries. I've got plenty in savings. I'm not the live-paycheck-to-paycheck type."

She snorted. "I sure am. Most people I know are."

"All the more reason that I'm the one footing the bill. Seriously, don't worry about it." He waved the key card over the sensor on the lock and pushed the door open to let her go inside first.

THE SUITE WAS CLEAN, as he'd predicted, with a kitchenette, a desk, a decent-sized living room with a cream-colored sectional and what had to be at least a 42-inch TV on the opposite wall. As he stepped in behind her, she checked out the bathroom, which was thankfully just as clean as the rest of the place. And the bedroom had two queen beds. That, at least, made her feel less guilty. Neither of them would get stuck on an uncomfortable pullout.

"It's nice," she said, turning around in the bedroom. "Oh." She had to take a step back, surprised to find him so close behind her.

"Sorry." He hefted her bag in the air in explanation. "I was going to set this on one of the beds so you can shower, if you want, and get ready for bed. I'll get ready after you."

She frowned. "Thanks. Where's your bag?"

He motioned toward the living room.

"No way." She pushed past him and grabbed his bag off the floor of the main room. "There are two perfectly good beds in this suite. You are not going to toss and turn all night on a lumpy pullout mattress." She headed back into the bedroom and plopped his bag on the second bed.

He spread his hands in surrender. "If you're sure."

"Of course I am. But I'll take you up on the offer to take a shower first. Do you need to use the bathroom before I hop in?"

"I'm fine. Go ahead. Want anything from room service? I'm going to order a hamburger or something."

Until he'd mentioned food, she hadn't realized just how hungry she was. She couldn't remember the last time she'd eaten something that hadn't come out of a vending machine.

"What time is it?" she asked, even as she reached in her pocket to check her phone.

"A little after one. I know it's way too late to eat, but I'm starving. I won't be able to sleep if I don't get something in my stomach besides potato chips and a candy bar."

She tossed her phone on the bed. "You read my mind. I'll have whatever you're having. Wait, do you think the hotel restaurant is even open this late? I bet room service is closed."

"If it is, I'll order pizza delivery. Pepperoni okay?"

"Sounds great. But a cheeseburger and fries would be way better. I hope room service is still open." With that, she disappeared into the bathroom with her bag.

She showered as quickly as she could, since it was already so late. She didn't bother to do more than towel dry her hair and comb it, and she figured there was no point in bothering with makeup. She'd just have to take it off to go to bed, anyway. It wasn't like Blake cared. Getting fully dressed seemed like too much effort, as well. And she didn't have that many clean outfits. So she decided to wear what she normally wore—a long nightshirt that fell to her knees and underwear.

The one concession she made was to keep a bra on. Not because she thought he'd even notice if she didn't wear one. But she didn't think she could take the embarrassment of him *not* noticing. A girl could only be ignored by the man she was half in love with for so long before dying of humiliation.

The delicious smell of cheeseburgers when

she opened the bathroom door nearly made her weep. She hurried into the living room and pressed her hand over her heart when she saw the two trays on the table—fully loaded cheeseburgers and thick steak fries, with two cans of Diet Coke.

"I think I've died and gone to heaven," she said. "How did you get these? I saw a notice on the bathroom door about checkout and room service times. They closed hours ago." She turned around then froze.

Blake must have risen from the couch when she stepped into the room, but that was as far as he'd gotten. His mouth had fallen open, and his gaze had fallen, too—from her lips to her breasts, lower, and lower still, until he was staring at her legs. His Adam's apple bobbed in his throat, but no sound emerged.

Fearing she'd done something stupid—like leaving the end of her shirt tucked into the top of her panties, she looked down, turning left and right to make sure the back was okay, too. Nope, thankfully, everything was covered. So what was his problem? She glanced up, then sucked in a sharp breath.

He'd crossed the room and was standing directly in front of her, looking so hungry it had her pulse rushing in her ears. She licked her lips and watched his eyes track the movement.

"Blake?" Her voice was hoarse. She thought she was reading the signs right, that he'd finally noticed she was a woman. But she was afraid to make any moves without being sure. "Are you hungry for the cheeseburger? Or…me?"

His gaze shot to hers. "What cheeseburger?"

"Oh, thank God," she whispered, just before he swooped down and pressed his lips to hers.

If the smell of the cheeseburger had been heaven, the feel of Blake's lips on hers was in a whole other dimension. He kissed her deeply, thoroughly, masterfully, until she was groaning against him, her fingers curling in his shirt, and her legs somehow curled around his waist, pulling him tightly against her. She didn't even remember him picking her up, but he must have. One of his hands cupped her bottom. The other clasped the back of her head as he pressed her against the wall beside the table.

They were both gasping for air when he broke the kiss. But he didn't stop, didn't even slow down his assault on her senses. He lightly nipped her neck, worshiped the top swells of her breasts with his lips and tongue. She threw her head back, and her lips parted on a sigh as she moved restlessly against him.

She'd wanted this—wanted him—for so long. She'd dreamed of being held in his arms. But even in her fantasies, actually being touched by him, feeling his warm hand roam beneath her shirt and against her skin, made her fantasies seem like black-and-white Polaroids compared to high-definition color. Blake the man was so much better than Blake the dream.

"Donna?"

The sound of her name whispered in deep, husky tones next to her ear sent shivers up her spine. She arched against him, reveling in the feel of his hard chest pressed to hers. He shuddered and tightened his hand on her bottom. Then he swiveled his hips in a sinfully delicious way that had her breath catching in her throat.

"Do that again," she urged.

He did, and she almost climaxed right there in his arms, both of them still dressed. Or, at least, he was. Her night shirt and bra had both been pushed up above her breasts, leaving them exposed to his wandering hands and lips.

"I want to feel your skin against mine," she whispered. "You have too many clothes on."

He swallowed and rested his forehead against hers. A shaky breath stuttered between his lips. "Are you sure you want this?"

For the first time since he'd kissed her, she opened her eyes. He'd pulled back just enough to meet her gaze, and the intensity of his hungry stare nearly made her weep with joy. Finally, finally, he was as desperate for her as she'd been for him for so very, very long.

"If you stop right now, I'm going to shoot you. How's that for being sure?"

His mouth tilted in a devastating smile. Then he was kissing her again, and she was kissing him back, their tongues tangling against each other in perfect rhythm, giving and taking, sharing, enjoying, until she wanted to weep from the beauty of it.

She was vaguely aware of him lifting his thigh to support her bottom dropping his hands from around her. Then crackling, like the wrapper on a pack of crackers. A tug, the sound of a zipper.

Her eyes flew open, and she looked down. She realized what he was doing, and was shocked that she'd never even thought of protection. Thank goodness he had. He must have had a condom in his wallet. And he'd cared enough about her to ensure that he didn't forget, even when she did.

She kissed him again and rolled the condom onto him. He shuddered and thrust his tongue deep inside her mouth, as he thrust his length between her hands. A very impressive length. By the time she'd finished, they were both panting and sweating and so eager that she helped him fit himself to her without even worrying about trying to stumble to the bed.

Then he was inside her, filling her, loving her. And she was loving him back, giving and taking, her entire body straining to get as close as possible to this handsome, strong, brave, intelligent man, who had finally had the sense to realize they could be great together—in every way.

Just when she thought it couldn't feel any better, he'd do something wicked with his mouth, his hands, his hips, and take her to a new height. She tried to give him as much pleasure as he was giving her, but he was a master at this, like he'd been created with the express purpose of giving a woman pleasure.

"Blake," she moaned, raking her nails across his neck. "Please."

He didn't have to ask what she was begging for. He knew. And he delivered. His hand moved between them and he stroked her, caressed her as he thrust in and out of her, making her gasp and make all kinds of strange, mewling noises she'd never known she could make. When her climax came, she would have shouted loud enough to wake the entire floor if his mouth hadn't been fastened to hers. He wasn't far behind, his entire body tightening against hers, his own groan sounding deep in his throat as he tumbled over the edge.

HE SHOULD HAVE let Donna sleep, but Blake couldn't seem to keep himself from touching her, sliding his fingers across the flat warmth of her belly and up to caress the underside of her full, perfect breasts.

He watched her roll over in the bed, little more than a shadow in the dark hotel room, as she wrapped her arms behind his neck.

"Hey, handsome." Her words were slurred, heavy with sleep.

"Hey, gorgeous." He pressed a kiss against the top of her head. "I'm sorry I woke you. Go back to sleep."

She yawned and pressed him onto his back, slipping her thigh over the top of his as she snuggled against him. "This is nice."

He rubbed his thumb against her nipple, delighting in how it hardened at his touch. "Yes. It certainly is."

She giggled and slapped his hand away. "I thought you were going to let me sleep. What time is it?"

"Early. Late. Take your pick. We both need to get some sleep, or we won't be able to function in the morning. But you're far too tempting. I'll go to the other bed."

He started to pull away, but she tugged him back.

"No way," she said, sounding more awake

than a moment ago. "I've got you exactly where I want you. Finally. You're not going anywhere."

Finally? Was it possible that she'd been wanting him all this time that he'd been wanting her?

She pulled herself up his body and pressed a kiss against the hollow of his throat. "Please tell me you have another condom."

He shook his head, even though she probably couldn't see him. "Sorry. I didn't plan this. I only had one."

She let her forehead drop against his chest. "You're killing me."

He feathered his hands through her hair and pulled her against him, pressing her head to his chest. "Trust me. The feeling is mutual. I really should move to the other bed."

"No. You woke me up. You have to pay the price."

"But I don't have any more protection."

"Then you'll have to pay it another way."

His body jerked against her at the thought of all the ways he could pleasure her. Eager to get started, he rolled her onto her back and began to work his way down to the very core of her. When his lips kissed her there, she bolted upright and grabbed his shoulders. She let out a shaky breath and was laughing when she pulled him up her body.

"As much as I'd love for you to do that," she

said, "I'm not that selfish. I'd want you to have as much pleasure as me, and honestly, I'm just too exhausted to do that right now."

He swallowed hard just at the thought of her doing that. But, sadly, it was not to be. Not today, anyway.

"Then I guess it's goodnight." He kissed her lips this time, and then he lay back and spooned himself behind her. In spite of how hard and aching his body was right now, being this close to her, the pleasure of just being able to hold her like this was more than adequate compensation. He was in awe that she'd let him make love to her.

"You're not going to sleep just yet," she said. "You still have to make it up to me for not having enough…uh…protection with you."

He frowned. "How do you want me to make it up to you?"

"Answer some questions."

"Questions? You want to talk? At…" He leaned back to get a look at the bedside clock. "Three in the morning?"

"We just made love. The least you can do is answer some burning questions I've had for a long time."

He sighed, growing sleepy as he snuggled against her. "What do you want to know?"

"Everything. Where were you born? Where

did you grow up? How many brothers and sisters do you have? Have you ever been married, had kids, pets—"

He cupped his hand over her mouth, laughing. "That's a lot of questions. If you don't draw a breath and let me answer a few, I'll forget them all."

"I'm waiting."

He chuckled again, and lightly ran his hand up and down her arm. "Let's see. Sadly, I'm not a Tennessee native. I was born in Alaska."

"That's cool." She giggled. "Literally."

"Clever girl," he teased, unable to resist pressing a kiss against her shoulder. "My family—all three brothers and two sisters of them, plus Mom and Dad—still live there, in Anchorage. They have acreage outside town. All of them built houses next to each other."

She turned toward him, even though he knew that she couldn't really see his expression in the dark.

"But you left? How old were you?"

"Eighteen."

"Then you…your family, you didn't get along with them? Did something bad happen?"

"No, not at all. I love my family very much, even visit them a couple of times a year. But I wanted to explore, see what else was out there before I settled down in one place. So I joined the navy, traveled the world and ended up in Knoxville of all places. I'm sure you'll be shocked to realize I wasn't keen on authority. I think it's because I was the middle child, with older brothers who tried—unsuccessfully—to boss me around all the time, and younger sisters I felt that I had to protect from being picked on by my brothers. I was always getting pulled one way or the other. You'd think I'd have become a peacemaker, an arbitrator between them. Instead, I just learned to fight really well. That's some of the appeal of the military—I got to fight the enemy. But I got in some pretty tight spots, so I decided not to make a long-term career of it. Went to college on the government's dime, and realized I actually missed the structure of the military. But not enough to sign up again. So I did the next best thing."

"You became a cop."

"Exactly." He slid his fingers through her hair, enjoying the silky, soft feel of it. "It's been an interesting career. Rewarding. But I've never really fit in. Dillon was right when he said I wasn't a team player. And Grant was right, too, when he told you I had…issues in Knoxville. What did he call them? Anger management problems? That's probably accurate. I punched one of my coworkers."

She surprised him by laughing. "Who hasn't?

I mean, I haven't. But I'm a woman, and we tend to be smarter than men. We solve our problems without having to hit each other."

"Gee. Thanks."

She laughed again. "Maybe it's a Southern thing. I don't know. But most of the guys I grew up with, and even the ones who are adults now—like Dillon—have punched other guys at some point in their lives. I don't personally think that's a cardinal sin like some people. As long as you can move on afterward, it lets off steam. Guys can do that—get mad at each other, have a knock-down, drag-out fight, then be fine the next day. I don't know how you do it. But it works. What happened? Your boss threatened to fire you over it, like Grant said?"

"Yeah, he did. If it had been anyone else on the team, he'd have said they deserved it. The guy I punched had just shoved a woman. And I didn't personally think he should treat one with such disrespect, no matter what occupation she had."

"Prostitute."

"Yes."

"Then good for you for punching him. It's not like women in that situation do it for fun. Life has usually beaten them down, and they get in a cycle of abuse or addiction. They should be given our empathy and be helped, not criticized or made to feel worse than they already do."

"You're a kind woman, and perceptive. Most people I've met wouldn't feel that way."

"Then they're idiots. You said if it had been someone else, you wouldn't have gotten in trouble. Was it the boss's son?"

"Nephew."

She snorted. "Jerk. He should be the one who got fired."

"I didn't get fired. I quit."

"Okay, right. You quit. And Chief Thornton hired you. How did that happen?"

"He was in town to visit someone he knew, an old-timer getting ready to retire. I gather they worked together years ago. Thankfully for me, he happened to be in the squad room when the whole altercation happened. Apparently the old-timer felt the way I did about the nephew and what he'd done. He talked to Thornton about me, and the next thing I knew, he'd offered me a job. In Destiny, I'd still be a detective, in my adopted home state of Tennessee, and I'd get to become a part-time SWAT officer, something I'd wanted for years. It was a no-brainer."

He feathered his fingers through her hair again, still in awe that he was holding her like this. Holding her, loving her, had been more than he'd ever dreamed he'd get a chance to do.

If he could change anything, the only thing he would change would be to keep the lights on after she'd fallen asleep in his arms in the living room and he'd carried her to the bed. He would have loved to just lie here all night staring at her beautiful face, seeing the way the light glinted off her glossy blond hair.

"Okay," he said. "I'm ready for more questions. Fire away." He smoothed her hair down and waited. "Donna?"

A soft snuffle, like a tiny cat puffing out a burst of air, sounded from her lips. Then she let out a decidedly unladylike snore.

He laughed and hugged her close. She'd accused him of snoring, when she was the one who snored. He couldn't wait to tease her about it. But for now, he'd have to wait. She really was worn out. They both were, and both needed their sleep.

As he settled down beside her and tucked the blanket around both of them, a feeling of guilt tightened his chest. Things weren't looking good for him to ever be a cop in Destiny again. Which was fine. He could go somewhere else, as long as it was in his beloved Tennessee. But Donna, well, she'd been born in Destiny and grew up there. Her family was there. He didn't have to ask her burning questions to know that. He'd been working with her for months and had simply listened. She'd freely spoken about her family, her hopes, her dreams. And all of them centered on living in Destiny. Could he ask her to give that up, to go somewhere else? The answer wasn't something he even had to think about. She'd be miserable anywhere but Destiny.

Which meant there was zero chance of them having a future together.

Worse, though, than the guilt he felt for basically having taken advantage of Donna in her sleep-deprived state was the realization of how the clock was ticking down for his fellow SWAT team members. They'd been missing for a few days. How many kidnap victims had been held that long and were returned alive and unharmed? He didn't know the statistics but imagined they were pretty dismal. Tomorrow, he and Donna needed to go full steam ahead and do everything in their power to find their friends. Because it was feeling very much like no one else was looking for them.

The clock was ticking. And it was counting down.

Chapter Thirteen

Being shy had never been in Donna's nature. Maybe being the oldest of four girls did that to a person. She'd been both friend and mother hen from a very young age, and had never had time to be shy. She was too busy making sure her younger sisters didn't kill themselves getting into something at school, or after school, before Mom and Dad came home from work. But this morning, she could barely look at Blake without feeling heat rise in her cheeks.

Not because she was embarrassed over what they'd done last night—which was probably what he thought. But because she couldn't seem to quit thinking about every kiss, every sweep of his tongue across her heated skin, every thrust of his body into hers. And she was so turned on, she was afraid that if she stared at him too long, she was going to jump him—condom or no condom.

So she showered, dressed and then ate her

room-service breakfast of toast and juice on the far end of the sectional sofa while he sat at the table, poring over the files they'd brought with them. She could feel his occasional glances and questioning looks. But she was careful to pretend complete fascination with her food rather than face the elephant in the room. If he unsettled her this much after making love, how was she even going to function today? Somehow she needed to turn her thoughts. And what better way to turn them than to work on the case?

He'd spoken on the plane about possibly visiting Sanchez in prison. But she wasn't confident that talking to a drug lord was worth their time. If he'd ordered the murder and kidnapping, he had no incentive to admit it. And it could be dangerous for Blake and her if he had someone powerful pulling strings for him, and keeping tabs on his visitors.

It could even be the FBI.

On the surface, the feds being in Sanchez's pocket didn't make sense. After all, they were the ones who'd spent a couple of years infiltrating his operation to build a case against him. Why would Grant, or his direct reports, do anything to jeopardize all that hard work? And what did it have to do with Destiny's SWAT team? The connections were there, right in front of her. But she couldn't quite make them fit. Still, she knew in her bones that they really did fit somehow. She just needed the right information, that one piece of data, to make the picture come into focus. Which meant she needed information about Grant. How convenient that they were in the town where he lived?

She grabbed her phone and surfed the web. She was both shocked and pleased at how easy it was to obtain the information that she needed.

Typically, if a simple Google search didn't reveal someone's home address, then social media was the way to go to. People posted all kinds of personal details online, never realizing just how much of themselves they were exposing to strangers who might use those details against them. And Grant, surprisingly, was no exception.

Oh, he was smart enough to have an unlisted phone number and had managed to keep his address unlisted in the usual places. And he didn't have any social media accounts that Donna could find. Even his wife and kids didn't seem to have any social media accounts.

But their friends did.

Just a few advanced searches led Donna from Richard Grant to his wife and two daughters via his daughters' friends, who posted plenty on social media—including pictures the entire world could see. Pictures of birthday parties at the Grant family home, pictures of the girls leaning against a boy's car in the street out front, conveniently right by a street sign and a mailbox. That was the money shot—giving Donna the exact address of Grant's home.

She used the map feature on her web browser to zero in on the location for a street view. Her tongue almost fell out of her mouth when she got her first good look at both the property and the house itself. Holy cow.

The agent lived in west Knoxville, in a neighborhood that wound through gently rolling hills, where every home had an expansive, manicured lawn. The subdivision—if you could even call something so grand such a common name— was an eclectic mix of Craftsman bungalows, sprawling Colonial Revivals, Tudors and even ranch homes. Some were large, some were small, all were expensive. A beautiful lake— Fort Loudon Lake—sparkled in the distance. And every driveway seemed to boast a BMW, a Mercedes or some other expensive car she couldn't even name.

Grant's home wasn't mansion-sized like many of the others. But it wasn't a shack either. It was probably a little over three-thousand square feet. It was one-and-a-half stories, likely with a couple of bedrooms and a bath on the second floor. But it was the first floor that took Donna's breath away. The facade was made of stacked stone and cedar shakes, with entire walls of fancy windows with boxes overflowing with luscious pink flowers. The grass was deep green and looked as if it had been groomed with a pair of scissors.

"You look like you're ready to drool," Blake's deep voice broke into her thoughts from across the room. "What has you so fascinated?"

"SSA Grant's home. Ever heard of a neighborhood called Sequoyah Hills?"

"Sequoyah Hills? That's where he lives?"

"Yep."

"The average FBI agent makes under a hundred-thousand dollars a year. At Grant's level, he makes somewhere under two, probably closer to one-thirty or one-forty. How can he afford to live in Sequoyah Hills?"

"That's what I was wondering."

He'd crossed the room and was now sitting beside her, looking over her shoulder at the street-level picture of the agent's home. "You sure that's his?"

"Positive. It took an enormous amount of dedicated research to find it, but I did."

"Ten minutes on social media?"

She grinned. "Five. You think he's on the take? Maybe Sanchez is paying him under the table to look the other way or purposely foul up the trial."

He shook his head. "I wouldn't conclude that based on the house. The bureau knows where he lives. I guarantee they would have made sure they knew where the money came from to buy it. Is he married?"

"He has the required wife and two kids, yes. Daughters—both teenagers."

"Then either his wife has one heck of a well-paying job, or they got their money the old-fashioned way. They inherited it."

"Maybe. I'm not convinced that he isn't dirty," she said.

"I didn't say he wasn't dirty. I just don't think this is about money. He's too smart to flaunt ill-gotten gains in public." He waved toward the house on her screen. "And I've been looking into him this morning, too. He's squeaky clean, the very image of the perfect FBI agent. Literally the only thing questionable that I've been able to find is this Sanchez trial postponement and the way he's treated you and me. Something happened recently that is weighing on him, forcing him to make some questionable decisions. We need to figure out what that recent event or situation is so we can follow the trail to whoever is holding our friends."

"Our friends? Not my friends?"

He let out a deep sigh. "Our friends. I miss them, and I never thought that would happen. Even Dillon, if you can believe it."

"I believe it. I'm not even surprised. I knew we were all growing on you. It was just a matter of time until you realized it yourself. Back in the chief's office, when Grant was asking about our impressions of the ransom note, you said 'that's not how we talk.' You didn't say *I talk*. You said *we*. That's when I knew you were one of us, part of the team. You just hadn't realized it yet."

"You got all that from the word *we*?"

She shrugged.

"Maybe you're right," he admitted. "But right now, we need to focus on bringing our friends home."

"Which is why we're checking out of the hotel and taking a road trip." She turned to face him. "We're going to break into Grant's home."

THIS TIME, IT was Blake's turn to be so shocked that his mouth literally fell open, just as Donna's had done in the chief's office, when Grant basically accused them of lying.

To be fair, they were.

He cleared his throat and scrubbed his face as if the lunacy of her statement could be wiped away just as easily. Nope. She was standing in front of him, a determined look on her face, fully prepared to argue her outrageous point. And it was definitely outrageous.

"Why?" he asked. It was all he could manage at the moment.

"Because he's wrapped up in this somehow. And it's not like we can ask him any questions. A guy like that, no question he's got a home office. And where there's an office, there are files and to-do lists and calendars and any number of things that might provide a clue that will make all of this make sense."

"So you *want* to go to prison?"

She rolled her eyes. "We won't go to prison if we don't get caught."

"Sure, right. Because it would never occur to a supervisory special agent to have a security alarm at his home, with security cameras. And nosy neighbors who have to know he and his family are out of town. Yeah, sounds like a brilliant idea."

She crossed her arms. "That's the goal. Do you want to hear my plan?"

"By all means. Enlighten me. How do you propose we do this without attracting attention, getting caught on film, or getting caught, period?"

"First, stop being sarcastic. It's not helping."

"Forgive me. What was I thinking?"

Her eyes narrowed.

He held up his hands in surrender. "Okay, okay. Tell me the plan. I'll hold my snarky comments until the end."

She shook her head but continued. "One of the jobs I had while working my way through college was at a security company. They were an alarm system builder and distributor. You know how vegetable canning factories stop the lines and change the labels? Same product but they swap the outside of the cans for different brands?"

"Actually, no. I didn't realize they did that. Sounds like it should be illegal."

"I agree, but it isn't. Or, at least, it wasn't back when the security company used that example to help me understand what they did."

"They manufactured systems for other companies to sell and distribute under their own brands?"

"Exactly. I was one of their 1-800 operators who answered questions from prospective clients about the various components in the systems they sold. All the information was in the computer system, of course, so I just punched in their questions and up popped schematics and common questions and answers. But to make sure we knew the systems well enough so that we didn't sound like we were reading it off a screen, we were constantly in training. They demonstrated the systems, how to arm them, disarm them, ways to override them. Are you following?"

"Unfortunately, I am. You think you'll recognize the features of Grant's alarm system and be able to disarm it."

"I'm ninety-nine percent sure that I can, yes. The company that I worked for distributed alarms to ninety-nine percent of the market. Even if we get caught on camera, once we're inside, I can erase us from the system. No one will ever know we were there. In and out, no muss, no fuss."

"What about the neighbors?"

"It's just past typical morning rush hour. Most of them should be at work. But even if they aren't, all we have to do is act like we belong. Park in front, instead of down the block. Walk up to the front door as if we have every right to be there. As long as we don't act suspicious, no one will pay us any attention."

"Too risky. Someone could call the cops, especially if one of the neighbors is house-sitting. There are too many variables."

"We could stop at a uniform store and get some coveralls and tool belts, make it look like we're there to fix something. Everyone needs home repairs. We could walk around the outside of the house, pointing up at the roof, pretend we're figuring out the best approach to fix something. Actually, I really like that. We could get in the backyard that way without raising suspicions. And disabling the alarm out of sight of the neighbors is much less risky."

"No."

She put her hands on her hips. "No? Come on. It's a great plan. It's low risk the way I've thought it out."

"Absolutely not. We are not going to break into SSA Grant's home, and that's final."

Chapter Fourteen

"I can't believe you talked me into breaking into a federal agent's home." Blake shook his head in disgust.

"You're supposed to be pointing at the roof, not shaking your head." Donna scribbled fake notes on a clipboard as they stood by one of the pink-flowering dogwood trees about twenty feet from Grant's front door. The latex gloves they were both wearing weren't exactly work gloves to match the blue dungarees they'd worn as their disguise. But at least the gloves would ensure that they didn't leave any fingerprints. Hopefully no one would notice their hands and realize something was off.

Blake pointed. "Look. Shingles."

"It would help if you actually looked at the house when you point at it," she muttered.

His sigh could have knocked over a horse.

"We need to work on your choreography," she

said. "Come on. Let's head around back and get this over with."

The hammers and screwdrivers hanging from their tool belts jangled as they walked through the deep green, well-tended grass to the garage side of the house. There was no fence, which was both good and bad. Good, because they didn't have to worry about any locks. Bad, because it meant they weren't completely hidden from view. The neighbors behind the house and to one side had high privacy fences and large back yards, which helped. But if the neighbors were home in the house on the other side, they would see everything. For that reason, she insisted they keep up the same pretense in the backyard, pointing to the roof, the gutters, various parts of the house, as if they were performing some kind of inspection. On the back porch, she peeked through the glass. A security alarm keypad was just to the left of the door inside—its red light blinking in warning.

That's when she knew they were sunk.

"What's wrong?" he asked.

She stepped back and pretended to study the window to the left of the door. "What makes you think something's wrong?"

"Donna."

Her shoulders slumped. "Remember I told you

the company I worked for made ninety-nine per-cent of the alarms in this part of the country?"

"Yes."

"Grant bought the other one percent."

He blinked. "You can't disable the alarm."

"No. I can't."

His jaw tightened as he looked up at one of the many cameras they'd passed when they'd walked around the house.

"You might want to keep your head down," she said. "Since I won't be able to erase our ex-istence from the recordings."

He swore. "What kind of alarm system is it?"

"Does it matter?"

He stared at her, his patience obviously wear-ing thin.

"Okay, okay." She gave him the information. He pulled out his phone.

"What are you doing?" she asked.

"You're not the only one with a history." He scrolled through his contacts. "I've disarmed an alarm or two during my military days. And I have a friend who's probably dealt with that other one percent." He pressed the dial button and placed the phone to his ear.

She put her hands on her hips. "You couldn't have mentioned this at the hotel?"

"I didn't want to encourage your life of crime." He turned away from her. "Yeah, Jack. Hey. I know, I know. It's been forever. I should have called long before now."

She crossed her arms, shaking her head as he threw out alarm terminology even she had never heard before. As he spoke, he peered in windows and doors, studied the cameras, even followed what appeared to be a phone line to a utility box at the end of the house. He hung up the phone and then pried the panel open.

Donna followed him. "Just how long were you in the military?"

He ran his fingers down some cords in the box and shrugged. "Ten years. Why?"

"You said you were only in for a few years, that you didn't want to reenlist."

"No. I said I decided not to make a career out of it. You assumed I was only in for a few years." He pulled a screwdriver and wire cutters from his tool belt. His movements were sure and quick as he snipped here, rerouted there, cut the coating off some wires and twisted them together with another set.

"What exactly did you do in the military?" she asked, in awe of his calm demeanor as he meticulously destroyed an extremely expensive alarm system, all without it going off.

He snipped one more wire, then shut the

panel, before looking at her. "I'd tell you, but I'd have to kill you."

"Ha ha."

He shoved his tools back into his belt. "I bought us time, and not a whole lot of it. We need to be quick, in and out."

She followed him to the back door and reached for the screwdriver on her tool belt.

"You coming in?"

She jerked her head up. Blake was standing just inside the family room. The French door was standing wide open.

"How did you—"

He turned and headed down the hallway on the right side of the house. She shut the door and jogged to catch up to him. All the doors in the hall were open, which made finding the office easy. He disappeared into the last room on the right, and she was left to catch up yet again.

He plopped into the desk chair and scooted up to the computer sitting on the massive cherry wood desk. After turning on the monitor and tapping the keys, he shoved his chair back. "Unless you're a computer genius, we're not getting anything useful off his hard drive. It's password protected."

She pressed her hand to her heart. "You mean

they didn't teach you how to break encryption algorithms in spy school?"

He pulled open a desk drawer and rummaged inside.

She stared at him, waiting for a snarky comeback. It never came. "Blake?"

"Uh-huh?" He opened another drawer.

"Were you…were you a spy?"

He pulled out his phone, checked the time. "If my calculations are right, we have approximately fifteen more minutes before we have to be out of here. Shouldn't you be searching for this amazing evidence you expected to find?"

"You and I need to talk."

"Yeah. I know. Maybe later. Like, after we rescue our friends."

His reminder of what was at stake jarred her into action. Since they didn't have enough time to study and read everything, she grabbed a book bag from one of the daughters' bedrooms, choosing a grimy, stained one that she hoped wasn't sentimental in any way. They shoved an appointment book into the bag, a calendar with handwritten notes on it, and a couple of files that seemed related to the Sanchez case.

Blake checked his phone again. "Five minutes. Anywhere else you want to check?"

"This office appears to be just for the husband. What if his wife has an office, too? There might be something useful in there."

He nodded, and they hurried down the hallway, through the living room and kitchen, to the other side of the house. Sure enough, there was a matching office on this side with decidedly more feminine decorating. Just as in the other one, they found an appointment book. She added it to her collection and headed to a set of file cabinets near the window.

"No," Blake said, motioning for her to leave. "No time."

"But I just want to—"

"Donna. If we're not out in about one minute, the motion sensors will come back on and set the alarm off. We're out of time."

She reluctantly hurried out of the room, her fingers itching to search the files. Blake put his hand on the small of her back, urging her to run. They raced out the French doors and he shoved them closed behind them. The light on the alarm keypad, which had been green when they were inside, now switched to red. The alarm had just rearmed.

"Wow. We literally got out just in time." She drew a shuddering breath.

"Maybe, maybe not. Hurry." He grabbed her arm and yanked her with him in a dead run across the backyard to the garage side of the house, where they'd parked their car. He clicked the key fob, unlocking the doors. "Get in."

Her heart was slamming in her chest as she jumped into the passenger seat, dropping the book bag to the floor. A bead of sweat slid down the side of Blake's face as he backed the car down the driveway at a sedate pace. But he was constantly searching the mirrors, looking up and down the street. As soon as they were on the road, he accelerated to the end of the block and around the corner.

"You're going the wrong way," she said, snapping her seat belt into place.

"No. I'm going a different way. Just in case."

"In case what?"

As if on cue, sirens sounded behind them—from the direction of the street they'd just been on, zooming toward Grant's house. If they'd left the same way they'd come in, they'd have gone right past the police car, or cars, from the sound of it. There was no way of knowing if the police might have pulled them over.

Neither of them said anything as he skillfully wound his way out of the neighborhood while avoiding the police. And she didn't bother saying out loud what they both knew—they'd dodged a bullet, had almost gotten caught. If Blake hadn't forced her to leave when he had, they'd probably be in handcuffs right now. And how would that have helped their fellow SWAT team members?

"I wanted to go see Sanchez after this," he said as he headed up a ramp onto the interstate.

"Too risky. I think we should head straight to Destiny."

"My feelings exactly. My house is on the way into town, so I figure we can stop there, grab some lunch while we look over our ill-gotten gains. If we still feel the need to explore the Sanchez angle after that, I can call a friend at the Maloneyville Road detention facility and see if he has any useful information."

"Maloneyville?"

"Part of Knox County's prison system. That's most likely where Sanchez is being held for now, and it's where any visitors would go see him—assuming he's allowed visitors. As high profile as he is, they may have restricted him to visits only from his lawyer."

Chapter Fifteen

Two hours later, they were sitting at the expansive mahogany table in the kitchen section of Blake's loft-style house on the outskirts of Destiny. Their bellies were full from some sandwiches they'd grabbed at a deli along the way. And the case files and stolen appointment books and papers from Grant's house nearly covered the entire top of the table. They'd been reviewing them for the past hour.

Donna straightened in her chair, stretching, her joints popping.

Blake glanced up at the sound, then tossed his pen onto a file folder and sat back. "You okay? Can I get you anything?"

"A chiropractor would be nice. I feel like a human pretzel." She stood and stretched some more before moving to the group of couches that marked the living room area. "I've probably passed this barn a hundred times and never knew it looks like an übercool loft inside. How come I never knew you lived here?"

"You never asked."

Guilt flooded through her. "You're right. I didn't. None of us did. We should have, though. We should have worked harder to include you. All this time, I thought you were being stand-offish, stubborn, refusing to be part of the team. I never tried to look at it from your side, that maybe you never felt welcomed, so you didn't try to join us. I'm sorry, Blake. I really am."

He stood and headed toward her. His long legs ate up the distance between them, and he was suddenly in front of her, tilting up her chin to look at him.

"There's plenty of blame to go around," he said. "On both sides. My background, as you've seen today, is a bit…unusual. I had a hard time fitting in at the Knoxville office because I couldn't talk about my past. That same…diffi-culty…pretty much transferred here to Destiny."

"Your super-secret-spy past?" She wiggled her eyebrows.

"My top-secret past. Can we leave it at that?"

She slid her hands up the front of his chest to entwine them behind his neck. Or she would have, if she could reach that far. She had to set-tle for letting the tips of her fingers barely touch. He was deliciously tall.

"I can live with that," she said. "And you need to stop beating yourself up. The rest of us have lived here all our lives, pretty much. There are age differences between us. We didn't all have the same classes or graduate together. But we share the experience of growing up in Destiny. And you're the first person we've ever had to welcome onto our detective squad and SWAT team who wasn't from around here, an outsider. Even though we pride ourselves on being friendly and welcoming to strangers, we pretty much sucked in the welcoming department when we brought one onto our team. I just hope we get the chance to do better—with you on our team again."

He leaned down and kissed her, a soft kiss that was over almost as soon as it began. But it was so darn sweet, it made her want to weep.

She really had it bad for this man.

She smiled up at him. "What was that for?"

He shook his head, but even though he didn't answer her with words, she saw the truth in his eyes. The mutual understanding of what had gone wrong. The desire to make it right. The relief that he'd found someone who finally "got" him. She felt the same way and hoped he read the same emotions in her eyes as she stared up at him.

He made a sound deep in his throat that reminded her of a lion. Then he was kissing her again. Really kissing her this time. Kissing her until all the clichés she'd ever heard about came true—jelly knees, the room spinning, her heart crashing against her rib cage. When he pulled back, his breathing was ragged, and there was regret in his eyes.

"Blake?"

"I want you," he whispered. "But we need to get back to work."

Once again, she'd let her fascination with him push her off course. Shame and guilt flashed inside her, making her push out of his arms.

"You're right. I need to make some phone calls to double-check some of the entries in Mrs. Grant's appointment book. Then we can compare notes."

"Sounds good. I'm a visual person. I've got a whiteboard in my closet that I haven't used in a while. I'll bring it out here so we can write out what we have and try to make sense of it. I figured I'd call Doc Brookes too, talk to him about the autopsy and any samples he took. My last call to Officer Lynch yielded nothing new. The lab still hasn't returned any results from the samples that were collected. And the private lab Lynch sent your gloves to hasn't gotten the DNA results yet. It's supposed to take a few more days. They have a backlog, like most labs. So we're back with Brookes to try to get useful information about the scene. Maybe he can talk me through what he saw, smelled, any impressions, things that might not be reflected in that sanitized version of the autopsy we got to read."

"That sounds like a great idea. Did Lynch have any reports about the team's vehicles? Were any fingerprints found that didn't trace back to the them?"

"I'll call him back and find out. I'm going to call that prison contact of mine, too, see if Sanchez has had any visitors besides his lawyer. Doubtful, but it doesn't hurt to ask."

She nodded her agreement and grabbed the appointment book. Then she headed into the other room to make her calls while Blake got the whiteboard set up on top of the table, with it leaning against the wall behind it. After they both finished their calls, they gathered their notes and took turns adding bullets to the whiteboard. Blake's notes went to the left of a vertical line he'd drawn down the center. Donna's notes went to the right.

"I think we should read them out loud, then discuss them," she said. "Want to start with yours?"

"Sure." He read each bullet on the left side of the line.

"Randy Carter, deceased, C.O.D. massive organ failure, caused by multiple gunshot wounds, all from the same gun, nine-millimeter slugs. Traces of mud with mineral deposits on clothing. No fiber evidence.

"Chief Thornton, Dillon Gray, Chris Downing, Max Remington, missing.

"All fingerprints found on the teams' vehicles had been sorted through and identified. No leads resulted from that.

"No footprint evidence, other than at the barn, one partial. Assume washed away by the rain.

"Sanchez drug trial postponed same day SWAT team went missing, per SSA Grant's request.

"Colin Lopez, one of Grant's senior agents, has driven to Knoxville every day since a week before the trial was postponed, to visit Sanchez. Visits are always approximately five minutes in duration—"

"Wait," Donna stopped him. "Your prison contact told you that, about Lopez?"

He nodded.

"Does he know why Lopez goes there? And does Sanchez's lawyer know about it?"

"From what I was able to discern, the lawyer knows about the visits and is against them. But it's Sanchez who insists he wants to see Lopez. As to what is discussed, my source assumes it's Sanchez pulling the FBI's strings, being a jerk basically, making promises he's not keeping."

"Like promising to tell them information in return for a deal, to avoid the trial continuing?"

"Maybe. We're completely guessing here. It could be any number of things. We may need to try to talk to Sanchez after all, or Lopez."

She waved toward the board. "Okay, keep going. You can read my side, too."

"Grant's family allegedly went on vacation several days before the SWAT team disappeared.

"There were zero entries in either Mrs. Grant's planner or Mr. Grant's planner about a vacation.

"Mrs. Grant missed a hair appointment.

"Both daughters missed a dance recital that had been planned for months.

"Grant's family is NOT on vacation."

He arched a brow. "Missed appointments led you to conclude that the family isn't really on vacation? That seems like a stretch. What makes you believe that?"

"Roots."

"Roots? Like tree roots?"

She laughed. "Hair roots. His wife is a bottle blonde. I saw her pictures at the house, with dark roots."

"You're not a bottle blonde." His voice was husky.

Her face flamed hot. She cleared her throat. "The salon Mrs. Grant uses is expensive, exclusive and has a long waiting list. It takes months to get an appointment. According to the owner, their clients never cancel."

"Never?"

"So she said." She rolled her eyes. "Mrs. Grant has standing appointments every three months to do her roots. She's been going there for years and has never missed an appointment. She had one the day she supposedly left on vacation. An appointment she did not keep. And she never called the salon. They're very unhappy with her."

She waved at the board again. "Plus, I may not have children of my own, but I have nieces and nephews. And I know how parents are about recitals of any kind, especially dance. Having your kid in dance classes is really expensive. The lessons alone are outrageous, but add to that the cost of outfits, and it skyrockets. It's a tremendous investment of money and time. And it all leads up to the recitals. You don't miss recitals. Period."

He stared at the board, appearing deep in thought. Donna decided to read off a few more of the bullet points herself.

"A mysterious cruise was arranged for the wives of the SWAT team. They were the only ones who 'won' tickets, even though it was supposed to be a charity for law-enforcement families. The wives left the day before the SWAT team disappeared.

"Lopez used his influence to help the one-time charity set up the cruise, to get past city permitting issues.

"The ONLY law-enforcement families on the cruise were from Destiny, even though the cruise was arranged by a charity out of Knoxville…"

She stopped. It was her turn to frown and puzzle over what she was seeing.

"What is it?" Blake asked.

"The cruise. Lopez's involvement seems to connect it with Grant, like so much of whatever is going on. And it was obviously focused on the wives of our officers. But there's a different slant to this than everything else."

He stepped beside her, as if he could see what she was thinking if he looked at the clues from the same angle. "Go on."

"Randy was murdered, which proves whoever took the rest of the team hostage means business. They're dangerous, and they want us to know that, so we give in to their demands. Only, there haven't been any."

"Which doesn't make sense in a ransom case," he added.

"Right. We've already concluded that delay, diversion, misdirection seem to be the goals. But why? Our victimology, the timelines, haven't raised any red flags. There's no one that we can point to as having any immediate grudges against our team. At least, nothing recent that we've looked at. It doesn't seem like it was personal in any way." She turned to look at him. "I'm starting to think the kidnapping of our team is random."

He stared at her a long moment, then shook

his head. "Can't be. It was planned ahead of time in order for the note to be ready, and the team to have been taken so cleanly, with almost no evidence left behind."

"Well, yes," she said. "It was planned, but what I'm saying is that it could just as easily have been another group of cops, in another county, who were taken. They may have chosen Destiny because of the location alone. Lots of foothills and woods and long stretches of rural roads. Much easier to sneak up on someone out here, without witnesses, than in a city. Maybe our team was chosen because they checked off the boxes of whatever the kidnapper or kidnappers needed." She stepped to the board and wrote another bullet. *Choice of victims irrelevant—goal was to create a diversion for other law-enforcement. Diversion from what?*

She set the marker back on the tray and joined Blake again. "Other than getting lots of law-enforcement people working on the case, what did the kidnapping do? What concrete effect did it have?"

Blake slowly nodded, as if he was beginning to see her viewpoint. "The Sanchez trial. We keep coming back to that. The trial was postponed because of the kidnapping. Maybe that was the goal all along, to put the trial on hiatus. The victims, who the bad guys kidnapped, were irrelevant." His gaze shot to hers. "Not to us. I meant to the bad guys."

She gave him a sad smile. "I knew what you meant. In addition to postponing the trial, the kidnapping got the main witnesses, the FBI agents who gathered the evidence against Sanchez, out of town, and temporarily out of the picture."

"Seems like it. The dates," he said, going to the board and tapping on the dates they'd written next to several of the bullets. "They all line up. Mrs. Grant and her kids left town a little before our guys were taken. The wives of the kidnapped officers were sent out of town around that same time. What did that accomplish? It got the women and children out of harm's way. That's the only thing I can think of. But do you know of any drug lord who would care about collateral damage? I sure don't. Which leads us back to one person who seems knee deep in this thing who might have known what was going to happen ahead of time and cared enough to protect them."

"Grant," she said. "Which is double damning against him because the families were sent out of town *before* the FBI was ever called."

He nodded. "He knew our guys were going to be kidnapped, and he wanted to make sure their families, and his, were kept safe."

"Safe." She fisted her hands at her sides. "Don't expect me to thank him when this is over because he went out of his way to keep the wives safe. He knew this was going to happen and did nothing to stop it, and Randy died because of it. I'm going to tear him apart with my bare hands once we have proof."

"I'll be right there with you," he agreed. "But we need to keep our eye on our goal—bringing back our team alive. So what else do we see?" He pointed to some bullets about the evidence at the lab. "If Grant is part of this, he's doing everything he can to buy time. That means doing things to hamper the investigation. Like sending evidence to the FBI lab when the state lab could have tested it by now and had the results back. He's interfering with the investigation."

"He totally is." She put her hands on her hips. "I have to believe the FBI, in a typical kidnapping investigation where the clock is ticking and time is of the essence, would put a rush on the test results."

"Who says they didn't?" He arched a brow. "For all we know, the results could be back, and Grant isn't sharing them."

She shook her head, incensed at the very thought. A man with the coveted position of supervisory special agent had turned on his fellow law-enforcement officers. He didn't care that one had died, and four more lives were in jeopardy. She was so upset she started shaking.

Blake's arm settled around her shoulders, drawing her close against him. "We're going to find them. Then we'll focus on making sure the FBI and others know what Grant has done. But we need to focus. With Grant driving the investigation, it's going in the wrong direction. We have to figure this out. Now."

She blew out a deep breath and put her arm around his waist, drawing on his warmth and strength to try to calm down and think. They both stood there for several minutes, quietly studying the board, silently reading through the dozens of clues and theories they'd written down.

"Mineral deposits." Donna frowned at the description that Blake had written about his phone call with Doc Brookes. "What did Brookes say about the mineral deposits on Randy's pants?"

"That the lab would have to test them to identify them. There were little pieces of grit mixed in with the mud. He said if he had to guess, he'd say it was either quartz or granite. The mud sparkled when he passed a light over it. That's the only reason he even noticed it."

She blinked and drew back. "The mud sparkled? Are you sure?"

"That's what he said. Why? Is there somewhere in Destiny with mud that sparkles?"

"As a matter of fact, there is. The old quarry. It's about a mile from Hawkins Ridge. It's been closed down for years, but they used to cut slabs of granite out of those hills. Between the bad economy and local environmentalists putting every roadblock up they could to stop the company from working there, they decided it wasn't worth the trouble and left. But I don't see how anyone could hide four people there. It's an open mine, kind of like with coal strip mining. They don't cut tunnels through the mountain like the other mines around here used to do when they were open. If they were at the quarry, someone should have seen them."

"If they searched that area, yes," Blake said. "But if Grant saw that in the report, and has any kind of geological map of the area to help with the search, he could have put two and two together way before we did and directed the search parties away from the quarry. Yet another stall tactic to drag this out."

"There's only one way to know for sure," she said. "We need to see whether the quarry was searched."

"I'll call Officer Lynch and see if he knows."

While Blake made the call, Donna waited, silently praying that this was it, the clue they needed in order to find the team. If Grant had steered the team away from searching that quarry, then that could be the red flag they were looking for. Because there was no other way she could think of for those sparkling mineral deposits to be on Randy's clothes. The kidnapper, the killer, must have trekked through the forest from that direction to sneak up on the SWAT team and transferred the granite chips from his own clothes to Randy. Then he took the team back with him, somehow. She didn't have a theory yet for how he'd done that without leaving any evidence.

The team could still be at the quarry—maybe tied up, or kept in some kind of shed or small building left over from the mining operation. If no one had searched the area, it wouldn't matter that it was an open mine. Kind of like the old philosophical question—if a tree fell in a forest, and no one was there to hear it, did it make a sound? Well, if a SWAT team was kept tied up in an open quarry, but no one was there to see them, did it really matter that the quarry was open? No. It didn't.

With the phone still to his ear, Blake moved to the table to one of the maps they had of the area. They'd marked off earlier spots as searched, based on previous calls to Lynch while on the plane. Now he marked off more spots, his mouth tightening into a hard line when he circled where the quarry should be.

Then checked it off.

Donna's shoulders slumped.

"Thanks, Officer Lynch," Blake said. "We both appreciate your help. Watch your back, okay? Neither of us trusts Grant, or any of the people he brought with him." A pause, then, "Soon, hopefully. We're working on some leads. Okay, we'll keep you posted, too. Thanks."

He hung up and slid the phone into his pocket. "They searched the quarry yesterday afternoon. Not because of any evidence, and not at Grant's direction. Some volunteers, along with the state police, decided to expand the search in that direction—even though Grant never asked them to."

He stared at the board another minute, then pulled his phone out again.

"Do you have another idea to follow up?" she asked.

He shook his head and punched in a number. "Other than going into the woods and searching on our own, no. I'm drawing a blank. But if this all revolves around Sanchez, I'm going to warn my friend at the detention center to beef up security. Maybe the delay was to give Sanchez a chance to try to escape when the focus wasn't on him and things weren't so hot. It's the only thing that I can think of at this point, even though there isn't any real evidence to back it up."

He made the call while Donna sat down and studied the map, checking all the places the teams had searched. They'd been thorough. Every building in a ten-mile radius of Hawkins Ridge had been checked. Did that mean the team had been taken somewhere else? In spite of the lack of tire tracks, had they been driven out of the county and were somewhere else entirely? If so, how were they going to find them?

"Donna."

The odd hitch in Blake's voice had her stomach dropping before she even looked at him. He'd put his phone away. And his brow was lined with worry.

"What happened?" she asked, dreading the answer.

"Sanchez attempted to escape a couple of hours ago."

She pressed a hand to her throat. "Was anyone hurt?"

"Two guards were killed."

She let out a ragged breath. "What about Sanchez?"

"They caught him. I don't have many specifics, but it seems like this must have been planned for months. It was an inside job. A group of new hires, hired when the trial first started, put everything in place to smuggle him out as one of the grounds crew members. It all hinged on him being transferred from the Knox County Jail downtown. He was at KCJ during the trial, but once it was postponed, he was transferred to the Maloneyville facility. Without that constant media attention anymore, or the extra vigilance at KCJ because of shuffling him back and forth to court, the heat died down, and guards began treating him like any other prisoner."

"Then what happened to Randy, and the others, *was* about Sanchez. The diversion was so everyone was looking the other way, so he could escape."

Her heart seemed to stutter in her chest as another thought occurred to her. "His plan failed. What does that mean for our team? If he doesn't need the diversion anymore, does that mean time has run out for our guys? Assuming he's kept them alive, now he has no need to worry about it anymore. He'll pull the plug on the operation. Or, if he can't get word out, one of his thugs will hear about the failed escape attempt on the news, and they'll know it's over. They'll cut their losses and run. We have to find our team now. It might already be too late."

He grabbed his keys from a hook on the wall

and pitched them to her. "You drive while I call everyone I know and tell them our suspicions about Grant and the link to Sanchez's escape attempt. We may not have enough proof to have him arrested, but with Sanchez having tried to escape, it gives a lot more weight to our belief that he's behind this, that he and Lopez colluded to make this happen. If nothing else, they'll want to interview Grant and Lopez to see if they know anything about Sanchez—and our men. That alone means we get someone else in to run the investigation."

She hurried to catch up to him as his long strides carried him to the door much faster than her shorter ones. "Where are we going? To the FBI field office in Knoxville to plead our case?"

He paused at the door. "We're going to Hawkins Ridge to search for them ourselves. Unless you have a better idea?"

She yanked open the door. "Let's go."

Chapter Sixteen

In spite of Officer Lynch's assurance that the quarry had already been searched, that was the first place that Donna and Blake decided to check—based on the mineral deposit evidence. Unfortunately, they didn't find their missing team. What they did find were lots of footprints from the searchers. If there had been any evidence of Sanchez's men out here, it had been obliterated. That was one of the problems with getting civilian volunteers involved—they lacked the training to preserve evidence.

Blake led the way through the forest, toward Hawkins Ridge. He held up a low-hanging branch for Donna to pass under, then took the lead again. When the woods near the top of the hill they were on thinned out, she joined him, and they walked side by side, studying the ground, scanning the woods, always on the alert in case anyone else was out here who shouldn't be.

When they reached the dilapidated barn, they both stopped at the closed double doors. A notice declaring it a sealed crime scene was taped across the middle.

Blake motioned to the notice. "What do you think?"

"I think I care more about searching for clues that might help me find my friends than preserving a crime scene."

"Exactly what I was thinking."

They both grabbed a handle and pulled the doors open, ripping the notice in half. The smell hit them immediately. Even with the body gone, the blood had soaked into the ground, and the place had been shut up without ventilation. It reeked of death.

Donna's face went pale. She blinked several times as if fighting back tears. But Blake knew it wasn't because of the odor, specifically. It was because of the memory of her friend, and what had happened to him.

"You can stay out here if you want," he said. "I'll look inside, see if there are any clues that didn't make it into the reports. You and I certainly didn't have time to properly search it ourselves when we were here last."

"No. We didn't. But I'm okay. I can handle this. The search will go faster with both of us."

She stepped in past him, scanning the floor and walls off to the right with her flashlight.

Blake did the same on the left side, but he couldn't help frequently glancing back at her to see how she was doing. He couldn't imagine how hard it must be for her to be here knowing that this was the place her friend had died. Knowing that her other friends could very well be dead, as well.

No, that wasn't entirely true. He was feeling some of those same emotions himself, to a lesser degree. He'd been thinking about his former team a lot ever since he was fired and they disappeared. And he'd begun to realize that they meant far more to him than he'd ever thought they could. But more than that, his emotions were all wrapped up in Donna, and his worry and concern for how this was affecting her. He wanted to protect her from every kind of hurt, every kind of pain, physical or mental. And he hated that he seemed helpless to do that right now.

They met in the center of the barn.

"Anything?" she asked.

He swept his light toward the row of stalls that ran across the back. "There are what look like fresh scrapes across the floor over there, most of them concentrated in one stall. But there aren't any hiding places. It's all open. Maybe the crime scene techs found some blood back there, or other evidence, and the scrapes are from their boots."

"Show me."

They went to the stall, and he pointed his light at the floor along the wall. "See those scrapes right there?"

She bent down and ran her fingers over them. "You're right. They're fresh. But there are old scrapes, too. Maybe a wild animal has been nesting in here—a raccoon or possum."

"And they were spooked by the search teams. Moved their nesting material somewhere else."

She straightened. "Maybe. Whatever, or who-ever, was here at one time is obviously not here now. We need to keep looking."

A couple of hours later, Blake paused in the parking area and turned in a slow circle. Donna was a good twenty feet away, slowly walking across the clearing, studying the dirt for clues. But Blake didn't think she'd find any. The lack of tire tracks and footprints from that night still baffled him. Even with all the rain, there should have been something to show that Dillon and the others had been here. No one was that good at covering their tracks—literally. Even if they'd gone back and tried to wipe them away, they'd have missed something. The area was just too large not to.

Donna crossed the clearing and stopped beside him. "What are you thinking?"

"Just…how impossible all of this is."

"Impossible? What do you mean?"

"The kidnappings. This parking area showed no tire tracks, even though we know that Dillon and the others—including you and me—were here that day. There are only two explanations that I can think of. Either the rain really did obliterate every single track, or the combination of rain and someone using, say, a rake, or something like that, purposely wiped away the tracks up here. The gravel road starts just a little farther down the mountain, so it wouldn't have been that difficult to do. There wouldn't have been an enormous area of dirt they had to worry about raking—again, assuming that's what they did to cover their tracks."

"Okay. Seems plausible not to have any tire tracks then. So where's the impossible part?" she asked.

"The road at the bottom of this mountain passes by several houses and a country store. But no one reported seeing any vehicles up here that day, other than the SWAT team's. We know they drove up here and never drove back down. But there's no evidence they were driven back down in another vehicle either. Like I said, no tire tracks of other vehicles, and no sightings by anyone who lives at the bottom of the mountain. That has to mean that the perpetrator or perpetrators didn't drive up here."

"Okay, I'm with you so far. Where does the impossible part come in?"

"The chief is a lot older and might have been easy to subdue. But the others—Dillon, Chris, Max, even Randy—were all young, in great shape. And they aren't exactly light. If someone snuck up here through the woods to surprise them, they wouldn't have been able to just carry them off somewhere, not without leaving some kind of trace. It's just not feasible. There would have been broken branches, footprints, something. So that means the team wasn't forcibly carried out of here."

He scrubbed his jaw and swept his arms out toward the woods surrounding them. "Did they walk out? Same problem exists with that scenario. Even if they'd been handcuffed, or tied up, and forced at gunpoint to walk through the woods to some other destination, they're not rookies. They'd know trackers would come in looking for them. They'd leave a trace of their passing in some way so we could follow them. I have zero doubt about that. Dillon and the others are just too smart not to have found a way. So all I can conclude is that they didn't walk down from this ridge. Which, of course, is impossible, too, because they're obviously not here."

She looked down the road, back toward the trees and then up at the sky, as if searching for answers there. "They couldn't have been lifted out by helicopter. This clearing isn't big enough to land one, and the team's vehicles were up here. There wasn't room. The trees are too thick. Could they have lifted the guys up into the chopper? Maybe it hovered?"

"No way," he said. "It was storming too bad that night. Thunder, lightning—too dangerous. Not to mention the heavy winds that blow down through these mountains in a storm like that. They didn't ride out of here in a vehicle. They didn't walk out of here. And they didn't fly out of here. So where does that leave us?"

Her eyes widened. "They're still here."

He nodded. "They have to be. But they're not anywhere that we can see. So they're—"

"Underground." Her voice rose with excitement. "The tunnels, from the old abandoned mines I mentioned earlier. They have to be in one of the tunnels."

"Tell me about those old mines. Would the openings to the shafts have been boarded up with warning signs? I don't recall seeing any during the paint ball exercise, or during our search today."

"I've never seen anything like that, and I grew up here. I remember my dad talking about the mines when I was little, and how clever the company was who created them. They were a lot more environmentally conscious than the owners of the quarry. They liked to conceal the openings with sheds that blended into the landscape and seemed as if they were a part of everyday life."

He grew still. "Sheds? What about old barns?"

They both took off running.

BLAKE SHOVED THE tire iron into the crack in the floor of the stall with the scratches they'd seen earlier, a crack that had taken him and Donna far too long to find. So long that they'd almost given up on their theory that the opening to a mine shaft might be hidden beneath the barn. Now, after searching for an opening in the floor, and then having to hike a mile to their rental car to get a tire iron and hike a mile back, they were on the verge of finding out if this was finally the end—or yet another disappointment in a long string of them.

He shoved the edge of the bar in farther, then pushed down on the other end. A loud click sounded, and a three-by-three square section of the floor popped up on one side, as if it were on springs. He dropped the tire iron and grabbed the edges, lifting to see what kind of tension might be on it. There was no tension. The floor swung up without a sound, and a dark hole was revealed below.

Donna aimed both her flashlight and her pistol down into the hole. A metal ladder was bolted into the side. There were six rungs, which led to a slightly sloping floor made of dirt. Thick timbers that were similar to old railroad ties shored up the hole. She moved her light all around. "Do you see what I see?"

"The dirt sparkles."

"It sure does. Well, partner? Obviously we're calling for backup at this point. But who do we call?"

He thought about it. "Lynch. I have no way of knowing whether the warnings I called in to my contacts have gone anywhere with the FBI. We can't risk bringing Grant in on this. And we have no way of knowing how far his corruption has gone—whether the state police are involved, too. The only people I trust to help us are the ones on our team, the Destiny police."

She grinned. "There's hope for you yet."

While Donna called Lynch and explained the need for secrecy, Blake edged forward on his stomach and leaned down into the hole. There appeared to be only one tunnel, or at least, in this part of the mine, there didn't appear to be any openings to other tunnels. And it appeared to go in a generally western direction, back toward the quarry.

"He's rounding up our guys," Donna said. "They'll make excuses and head out one or two at a time. A mass exodus might make Grant suspicious. Lynch thinks they'll be here in about half an hour."

He pulled back out of the hole and looked up at her. "Half an hour is too long. We have no way of knowing what Sanchez's people will do now that his escape attempt failed. I don't want to wait, especially if this ends up being a wild-goose chase and the team isn't down there."

She chewed her bottom lip. "Okay, okay. But let's do this by the book. Well, without the waiting for backup part. I'm your wingman. You're mine. We're each other's backup. No running off and leaving each other no matter how tempting. Agreed?"

Her little speech stung, but he couldn't fault her. The last time he was supposed to watch her back, he'd let her down. If it had been a true SWAT situation instead of an exercise, she could have been killed.

"Agreed. But I go first."

She frowned. "Why? Because I'm a woman?"

"Yes."

Her face flushed with anger.

He pulled her face close to his. "It has nothing to do with your abilities as a police officer. And it's not because you're *a* woman. It's because you're *the* woman, the one I care about. And I couldn't bear it if you got hurt. Call me a chauvinist or whatever you want. But those are my terms. Either I go into that hole first, or we don't go at all."

He punctuated his little speech by kissing her, a quick soft kiss that he hoped conveyed just how much she mattered to him.

She let out a soft sigh. "You're ruining me. I was a badass cop before I met you."

"You still are. The biggest and baddest around."

"It's too late for flattery." She waved toward the opening. "Go. Let's get down there and see what we find."

He braced his hands on both sides of the cut-out, swung his legs into the opening and dropped down onto the dirt below. He grabbed his flashlight and pistol and trained them in front of him, watching the shadows and listening. "Clear."

"Show-off," she muttered above him. "Must be nice to have long legs." Her shoes rang out against the metal ladder as she climbed down behind him. Her flashlight clicked on, adding more light to his. "Ready."

"Donna?"

"Yes?"

He looked over his shoulder at her. "Your legs are perfect just the way they are."

Her eyes widened, and he turned around so she wouldn't see his grin. "Let's go."

They moved quickly, without pretense of stealth. There really wasn't any point. Every little sound echoed in the tunnel. If there were any bad guys up ahead, they'd hear him and Donna coming a mile off.

A few minutes in, the tunnel ended at an intersection. They stopped and studied the ground.

"Footprints," she whispered, "down both tunnels. Split up?"

"No way," he said.

"Because I'm a woman again?"

"Because we're each other's wingman—wing person, people, whatever. We're not splitting up. That's what Dillon taught me, and what you taught me. We'll check the tunnel on the left first, then come back and check the other one, if that's what it takes."

A smile curved her lips. "I think my work here is done." Then she hurried down the left tunnel before he could stop her.

He cursed, hating that he'd fallen for her trick. "Come back here," he whispered. "I'm supposed to lead."

"My turn."

He bit back what he thought of that. The ground was softer here, their footfalls more muffled. Stealth was back on the table. Donna must have realized it, too, because she seemed to be making an effort to walk more softly and she didn't talk anymore.

Blake bided his time, keeping an eye out in front of them, just as much as he checked behind. He didn't want Donna running straight into an ambush.

The tunnel turned again, a sharp turn, and a light shone from up ahead.

They both flipped off their flashlights. Blake pulled her back, pressing both of them against the wall of the tunnel. They waited. When the light up ahead didn't move, he whispered, "Keep going or wait for backup?"

"I'm not waiting," she whispered.

He hadn't figured she would. He tapped her shoulder, and they both started forward, hands touching the wall on the left to guide them. Thirty feet, twenty, fifteen. The light was coming from some kind of chamber, probably an overhead light built into the tunnel ceiling. It definitely wasn't moving like a flashlight or lantern. And it was too bright not to be from a light fixture of some kind. When they were just a few yards shy of the opening, they stopped.

There was no way to see into the chamber without anyone in it seeing them at the same time. All they could do was go for it and hope for the best.

He wrapped both hands around his pistol. Donna did the same. There was enough light for them to see each other, so he mouthed the countdown.

Three.

Two.

One.

They ran into the chamber. Everything seemed to fill Blake's vision at once: tunnels opening off to the left and right of the cavern, the gunmen about forty feet in front of them, their teammates—Dillon, Chris, Max and the chief—caged like animals behind a wall of bars in the back left corner.

"Freeze, police," Blake shouted at the gunmen.

The rest seemed to happen in slow motion, and yet all at once. The gunmen swung their weapons toward the two of them. Blake shouted a warning at Donna and fired at the gunmen. One of them screamed and fell against the man beside him, clutching his middle. Another man went down, a split second after Donna's gun boomed next to Blake. There was nowhere to hide, no cover. It was all about speed, who could outshoot whom.

Bam, bam, bam! Donna and Blake crouched together, shoulder to shoulder, firing as if they were on a gun range, but with the knowledge that every shot counted, and lives were on the line. Not just their own, but the lives of their men.

It was over as quickly as it had begun. The sudden silence was almost as shocking as the deafening gunshots had been. Blake and Donna stood together, chests heaving, staring at the carnage in front of them. Six men lay dead on the ground.

He could hear her swallow hard beside him. "Are you okay?"

He kept his pistol pointed forward, just as she did, adrenaline still pumping through his system.

"Yes," she said. "You?"

"Your three o'clock!" Dillon's voice shouted from off to their left.

Blake and Donna jerked to their right, firing as one. *Bam, Bam, Bam!* Three more gunmen fell to the ground, dead.

Footsteps sounded from the tunnel to their left. Blake swung his pistol toward the opening. Lopez ran through it, gun in hand. His eyes widened when he saw Blake.

"Freeze," Blake shouted.

But Lopez didn't freeze. He swung his weapon toward Blake.

Boom! Bam!

They both fired. Lopez went down.

"Blake!" Donna yelled.

He jerked around, expecting to see more gunmen. He did. Just one. Lying on the ground a few feet from Donna.

"Lopez shot him," she said. "He was protecting me."

He whirled back around. Lopez was writhing on the floor, clutching his chest.

Blake swore and ran to him. He kicked Lopez's pistol away from his body and dropped down on one knee. After holstering his own gun, he ran his hands across Lopez's chest, searching for the wound. Lopez's lips were turning blue, but there didn't seem to be any blood.

Blake grabbed the edges of the man's shirt and ripped it open. Buttons went flying, pinging off the ground like pebbles.

Donna stood guard over both of them, scanning the tunnel openings with her pistol.

"He's got a vest on," Blake said. "He's just got the wind knocked out of him."

"Sit him up," Max called out. "Bend his knees."

"Like I care if the scum bucket dies," Blake

grumbled. He ignored the way Lopez's eyes widened with even more panic as he struggled to draw air, like a fish gasping its last after being plucked from the water and landing on the dock.

In spite of his overwhelming desire to punch the traitor, Blake did as Max suggested and helped the agent sit up. Blake shoved the man's legs up toward his chest, and could tell exactly when air rushed back into his struggling lungs. He gulped several times, like he couldn't quite get enough of the stuff. His lips lost their bluish tinge, and he finally let out a deep, shaky breath.

"Thank you," he said, still gasping.

"Don't thank me just yet," Blake said. "Tennessee has the death penalty. And I'm going to do everything I can to see you on death row for Randy's murder." Blake jerked him up to standing and whirled him around to handcuff him.

"Wait," Lopez cried out. "I'm not the one who killed your teammate. And I'm not the one who kidnapped your team."

"He's right about one thing," Dillon called out. "He didn't kill Randy. One of the guys you shot did."

For the first time since coming into the chamber, Blake looked directly at the cage that had been set up in the corner. Relief swept through him to see all four men standing at the bars, looking dirty and tired, but other than that, unharmed.

"Are you okay?" he asked, needing to hear it for himself.

"We'll be okay as soon as you let us out of here." Dillon motioned toward the other side of the chamber. "The keys are on a hook on that wall."

Donna retrieved the keys and let them out. All of them surrounded Lopez, who cowered against the wall, his eyes round with fear. But it was Dillon who spoke.

"After we were ambushed in the barn, and brought down here," Dillon said, "Lopez came here once a day and took our picture on a cell phone. Since the guys who were guarding us let him in and out, he's obviously working with them."

Lopez shook his head back and forth. "No, I'm not. I mean, kind of, yes. But I had no choice. And I was coming here tonight to save you. All of you."

Blake gave a harsh laugh. "You and what army? There were nine armed men in here."

"This army."

Blake whirled toward the sound of the voice coming from the tunnel where Lopez had emerged moments earlier.

"Whoa, whoa, hold it." The man raised his

hands high in the air. "Think carefully, son," he said. "I really don't think you want to shoot the director of the FBI."

Blake slowly lowered his gun, recognizing the man in the business suit standing there. "No, sir. I wouldn't." He holstered his gun, and motioned for Donna to do the same.

A dozen men filed out of the tunnel from behind the director.

The sound of more footsteps echoed in one of the tunnels behind them—the same tunnel from where Blake and Donna had emerged. Everyone drew their pistols, even the director, and aimed them at the opening to the tunnel.

Officer Lynch and half a dozen Destiny police officers burst from the tunnel, guns drawn.

"Hold your fire," Blake, Donna and the whole SWAT team yelled.

Everyone froze for several seconds, Lynch's eyes so wide, they looked like they might burst from his head.

"It's okay," Blake announced. "Everyone here is on the same team." He eyed Lopez. "Well, most of us." He motioned for Lynch and the other officers to holster their weapons. As soon as they did, the director's men did, too.

"Well, that was exciting." The director's voice was bland, with a hint of laughter in it. He stepped over to Blake. "Can I assume that you're

Detective Blake Sullivan? The one who called Maloneyville a few hours ago and warned them that Sanchez was going to try to escape? And then called half a dozen special agents, making an outrageous claim about Supervisory Special Agent Richard Grant being a dirty agent, who may have orchestrated the kidnapping of a SWAT team and the murder of one of the members of that team?"

He swallowed and cleared his throat. "Yes, sir. Guilty."

The director offered his hand. "On behalf of the FBI, I offer you my sincere apology for whatever the hell is going on. And I promise you, we'll get to the bottom of this. Together."

Blake stared at him in surprise then shook his hand. "I don't understand. How did you end up here? When I called, I didn't know where the team was being held."

The director motioned to Lopez. "I was in Knoxville for an FBI function, and one of the local field agents told me about your phone calls. A few minutes later, he patched a call to me from Lopez, saying he had a life and death situation on his hands and needed backup immediately—but that I couldn't tell Grant. He gave us the GPS coordinates of the entry to this tunnel, down by the quarry, and met us there."

"So there's another entrance," Donna said

from beside him. "We must have missed it when we were in the quarry."

"It's well hidden," the director said. "Not sure my men would have found it if Lopez hadn't been watching for us. And now that the crisis seems to be over, I think it's time that Special Agent Lopez told all of us what exactly is going on."

As one, the chief and the SWAT team stood in front of Lopez, shoulder-to-shoulder with the director, facing a sweating, terrified-looking Lopez as his gaze darted from one to the other.

Blake waited until Lopez was staring directly up at him. "Start talking."

Chapter Seventeen

Blake and Donna were given the honor of stepping into the police station first. It was a bittersweet victory, knowing what they now knew, to see SSA Grant turn around from speaking to one of the other agents and watch them walk through the doors. Dillon and the chief followed, then Chris and Max. And finally, the director, Lopez and the small army of special agents and Destiny police officers, who'd all been in the tunnels together.

What struck Blake was how unsurprised Grant looked to see them, as if he'd known his time had run out. It wasn't until he saw the director and his entourage that he went pale and his eyes widened in shock. No, that wasn't accurate either. He'd already been pale, alarmingly so. But he did seem to blanch when the most powerful man in the bureau strode toward him. All in all, the haggard, gaunt look to his features and the lack of surprise at seeing the

SWAT team went toward corroborating what Lopez had told them back in the mine.

"Director," Grant said. "What a…surprise to see you here, sir." He aimed a questioning look at Lopez. "What's going on?"

"Knock off the innocent act," the director told him. "Lopez told us everything. How Sanchez had armed men break into your home, holding your wife and daughters hostage with the threat of killing them if you didn't do exactly as he said. Lopez was there with you at the time, so he was looped in. But he warned you that if anyone else found out, you'd come home to a dead family."

Although it didn't seem possible, even more color washed from Grant's face, leaving his skin translucent.

The director continued. "In exchange for postponing the trial, you were to look the other way and allow the Destiny SWAT team to be taken hostage."

A chorus of grumblings erupted in the room, most of it coming from the Destiny police.

Chief Thornton raised a hand, and they quieted down.

The director nodded his thanks but didn't look away from Grant. "You didn't feel you had a choice. I know that. But because of your inaction, a man died. Detective Randy Carter."

Grant swallowed, looking miserable. But he didn't say anything.

"But you did do what you could to protect their families," the director allowed. "You and Lopez created a fake charity to ensure that the SWAT team members' wives were on a cruise, out of harm's way, when the team was kidnapped. And since you had negotiated a daily proof of life from Sanchez for your own family, after the SWAT team was taken, you negotiated daily proof of life for them, as well. Lopez was the go-between. He took a picture of the SWAT team every day and took it to Sanchez at the detention facility. In return, Sanchez would have a picture texted to Lopez's phone while he was there, a picture of your family."

Grant braced a hand on the desk closest to him, as if he was afraid he might fall without the support. "It was the only thing I knew to do, the only way to try to keep all of them safe—the Destiny SWAT team, and my family—until I could figure out how to resolve this, or find my family so I could organize their rescue. That's what I've been trying to do. But something happened. Sanchez's escape plan went wrong."

"Yes." The director's voice was harder now, no hint of the earlier empathy he'd had when talking about Grant's family being taken. "And two more police officers paid with their lives.

That's unconscionable, Richard. You should have called me. You should have trusted your team to have your back before this went too far. Before good men died."

Red heat flushed Grant's cheeks, and his spine stiffened. He let the desk go, his anger appearing to give him renewed strength. "It's easy to judge me." His eyes flashed as he looked at Donna and Blake, and the rest of the SWAT team, before meeting the director's gaze again. "And it's pathetically easy to say what I should have done, looking back. I argued with Sanchez, tried to reason with him. In the end, arranging that cruise, warning Sanchez not to hurt anyone—which I did—was the only thing I felt I could do. I was buying time while Lopez and I tried to find my family without Sanchez knowing we were searching for them. I never expected anyone to get killed. I was doing everything in my power to try to ensure just the opposite."

"You should know by now," the director said, "that you can't negotiate with criminals. That was your first mistake, believing that Sanchez would follow through on the deal that you made. Three men have paid the price for your poor choices. And if it wasn't for Detectives Blake Sullivan and Donna Waters, four more men would probably be dead right now." He waved to the chief and the others. Then he motioned to one of the FBI agents beside him. "Arrest SSA Grant, please. Put him in one of the holding cells I see at the back of the room."

"No, wait. Don't." Grant struggled with the strength of desperation. It took four men to subdue him and put him in handcuffs. "My family," he yelled, as they dragged him toward the cells. "You have to find them. Sanchez will have them killed!"

"I'll do everything in my power to keep that from happening," the director called out.

Grant swore viciously, but as soon as the cell door shut behind him, he collapsed onto the bunk, put his head in his hands and wept. He'd obviously given up all hope and believed his family was doomed.

"We have to find the mole," the director whispered to Blake and Donna. "Other than Lopez, who in here are his right hands, the ones who are around him the most? Agents who would know what Grant is doing at all times and could report that to Sanchez?"

Donna turned to Blake and frowned up at him. "This room always felt big until half the county pushed its way inside. Can you see over everyone's heads? Where are Joel Lawrence and Stacy Bell?"

Blake craned his neck—for once, his height

not helping a lot, since so many of the other men in the room were nearly just as tall. But then he spotted one of the agents. "There, in the back right corner. The agent talking to one of the Destiny police officers. That's Joel Lawrence. Grant introduced him as one of his longtime core team members. Where Grant is, he is for the most part. Him and Lopez, of course. And Stacy Bell."

The director spoke softly to one of his men, who then forced his way through the crowd to Lawrence.

Blake continued his slow circle, looking for the always smiling agent who'd offered her condolences over Randy's death to both him and Donna when they first arrived.

"She isn't here, is she?" Donna said, staring up at him.

"I don't think so."

Donna immediately turned away and threaded her way through the crowd. Blake was about to ask her what she was doing, but Dillon stepped in front of him.

"What's wrong?" Dillon asked.

"Someone's missing. One of Grant's direct reports, Stacy Bell. She's Caucasian, has shoulder-length brown hair, is about five foot four, maybe 110 pounds."

Dillon motioned to Max and Chris, who immediately headed to the doors and blocked them to ensure that no one went outside. Then Dillon and Blake walked the entire room, looking in the interview room, the chief's office, his private bathroom, the squad room's bathroom.

Blake winced as he passed Grant's cell. The man looked absolutely stricken. And he had a good right to be.

They returned to the director.

"The mole has to be Stacy Bell," Blake said. "But she's gone. She must have snuck out when we were confronting Grant."

The director briefly closed his eyes as if in pain. "When I was confronting Grant, you mean. I was so angry with him that I didn't secure the scene first. I should have posted someone at the doors. I should have—" He frowned. "What's that noise?"

The distinctive squawking of someone talking through a police radio sounded from a few desks over. Dillon and Blake cleared a path. Donna was sitting at the end of the second row, her handheld radio unit sitting on top of the desk, the sound turned up. It was plugged into one of the mobile switchboards the 911 operators used.

"Go ahead, Billy," she said. "Say that again?"

The room grew silent as everyone tried to figure out what was going on.

"I said no one's been down Brook Hollow Road all day," the voice came through the speaker. "I've been out here fishing. I would have noticed. The cars scare the fish."

"Okay, Billy. That takes care of all the routes north of town. Thanks."

"Anytime, Donna."

She punched some buttons on the mobile switchboard.

"Hello?" a woman's voice came through the radio speakers.

"Molly, hey, it's Officer Waters. I've got a situation here. A missing woman, about five foot four, brunette. She's not from around here and might be lost. She's probably driving a blue Toyota Corolla, late model. Have you seen anything like that in the past hour out your way?"

The director shook his head. "What is she doing?"

Blake grinned. Leave it to Donna to get the logistics of what Stacy might be driving and get to work to try to find her while the rest of them were still standing around, pondering their next steps.

"She's initiated a call tree," Blake said, unable to keep the pride out of his voice.

"A call what?"

"A call tree. It's Donna's version of an AMBER Alert, or a BOLO. But much more effective. Trust me. I know firsthand." He crossed his arms, smiling as he watched her.

The director didn't seem impressed. He motioned to another one of his men. "Get a team together. We need to organize roadblocks and get some volunteers out here to help us look…"

Blake tuned the director out and waited for Donna to work her magic.

Dillon stood beside him. "Firsthand, huh?"

"Long story."

"You can tell me about it later. Detective."

Blake shot him a surprised look. "Does that mean what I think it means?"

"I'm sure I don't know what you're asking. I never fired anyone, no matter what you might have heard."

"What about the chief, and the mayor? Grant told me that—"

"Leave the mayor to me." It was the chief this time who spoke from behind them. "Knowledge is power, and I've been around this town long enough to have plenty of knowledge. Don't you worry about your job, Blake. It's here for you. If you want it."

Blake smiled, and couldn't help looking at Donna, and what he hoped having his job back could mean as he replied, "Thanks. I do. Very much." He cleared his throat and looked at the chief. "That is, if the rule about officers not being allowed to fraternize with each other can be lifted."

The chief followed Blake's gaze to Donna and grinned. "I'm sure I can arrange that."

Dillon clasped Blake on the shoulder. "We'll be glad to have you on the team again. From what I've seen, you've learned a heck of a lot more about teamwork over the past week than I ever tried to teach you. Great job. And thanks for sending Ashley and the others into hiding, keeping them safe. Donna told me about that while you and the director were talking during the drive here. I imagine Ashley's keeping an eye on the news. As soon as the media gets a hold of this, and she hears we're safe, they'll all be back in town. I can't wait to see her again. And my little girl. It's been way too long since I held them in my arms."

Blake wrinkled his nose. "You might want to shower first."

Dillon gave him a good-natured shove.

"I heard we're down a man," a deep voice said behind them.

Dillon and Blake turned to see their former SWAT teammate who'd moved away when he'd gotten married, Colby Vale. His eyes were red-rimmed. Max and Chris flanked his sides, having obviously relinquished their door guarding duties to someone else.

Dillon grabbed Colby's shoulder and hauled him in for a hug that should have cracked his ribs.

Colby tightened his arms around Dillon, his eyes looking suspiciously wet when they broke apart. "I'm so sorry about Randy." His voice sounded raw.

"I know." Dillon grasped his shoulder again. "We all are."

"I've got it," Donna called out, jumping to her feet and waving a piece of paper. "I've got Stacy Bell's location." She read the address out loud.

Dillon exchanged a startled look with the rest of the team.

"What?" Blake asked. "You know that address?"

"You could say that." Dillon's face looked grim. "It was before your time, before you joined the team."

"Mind if I tag along?" Colby asked. "It would be my honor, for Randy."

Dillon nodded as Donna joined them. They all stood in a circle, and Dillon put his hand in the middle. "For Randy."

Max followed, placing his hand on top of Dillon's. "For Randy."

"For Randy," Chris said, slapping his hand down on theirs.

The chorus continued until all six of them—

Dillon, Chris, Max, Colby, Blake and Donna—
had joined hands in the middle. Then the chief
leaned in, tears unabashedly flowing down
his cheeks as he placed his hand on top. "For
Randy."

"Gear up, team," Dillon ordered. "Destiny,
Tennessee, SWAT has a job to do."

Chapter Eighteen

Blake crouched beside Dillon beneath the window, cradling his assault rifle. He and the rest of the six-person SWAT team waited for the green light to begin the rescue operation in the one-story office building of Gibson and Gibson Financial Services.

Once again, the team stood ready, in the same spot where they'd rescued Ashley a few years earlier at a workplace shooting. Or so they'd told Blake on the way over here. That original mission was referred to as Tennessee Takedown.

But today, they were there to rescue someone else—a mother and her two teenage daughters. And the team had a brand-new member—Blake, who finally, for the first time, felt like he really belonged. Randy was there, too, in spirit. And they were all anxious to get inside and do their job.

Beside Dillon, his friend since childhood, Chris Downing, watched the screen on his wristband, showing surveillance from the tiny scope he'd raised up to the window.

"Casualty at three o'clock," he whispered into the tiny mic attached to his helmet. "Appears to be the security guard. No sign of anyone else."

The building had been abandoned since the shooting that had nearly claimed Ashley's life. The owner of the building had told them that there was one guard who kept an eye on the place, until he could find a buyer. The chief had asked the owner to try to contact the guard to warn him. But he couldn't get through, even though he'd called a dozen times. Now they knew why.

Blake's earpiece crackled, and the chief's voice came on the line. "Witness says there might be two shooters—Special Agent Stacy Bell and one other, possibly the man assigned by Sanchez to watch the family. No descriptions of weapons. Be extra vigilant."

"Do we have the go-ahead to move in?" Blake asked, inching closer to the door.

Dillon arched a brow and spoke into the mic. "Chief?"

Thornton practically growled through the headset. "Like you're going to follow my orders either way? Just handle it, Dillon."

Dillon grinned, as did the rest of the team. Donna laughed.

Blake stared at her, wondering if she and the others had gone crazy. "Is there something I should know about?"

"Inside joke," Donna said.

Blake tightened his hold on his gun, and wondered if maybe he'd been wrong earlier in thinking he was part of the team now.

"Blake?" Donna said. "We ignored Thornton's direct orders the last time we were crouched under this very window. That's why I laughed. That's why everyone was smiling, and Thornton sounds like a grumpy bear."

"Don't push me, Officer Waters," Thornton growled again through the headset.

Donna grinned and winked at Blake.

That wink was like a jolt of electricity, shooting straight through his body, warming him from the inside out. It blasted away his doubts, and it had him wanting more than ever to finally get Donna alone and tell her all the things that had been going through his head since the moment he realized that he wasn't leaving Destiny. Or, at least, he didn't want to. But Donna was the one who would be deciding his fate.

Whether she realized it or not.

Chris tapped Dillon's shoulder. "Movement on the east corner," he whispered. "Appears to be a civilian. Belly-crawling toward the exit. I think it's one of the daughters."

"Is she hurt?" Dillon's questioning gaze drilled into Chris.

"Negative. I don't see any signs of injuries." He smiled. "Not like last time, huh?"

Relief flashed across Dillon's face. "Not so far. Let's do this. Let's bring these people home. No casualties today, team. You got that? I don't want anyone hurt but the bad guys. And not even them if we can help it." He motioned to Blake.

Blake jerked the door open, and the team rushed inside, two by two, pausing just past the doorway as they scanned the expansive rows of cubicles with their rifles.

Dillon pointed to the young girl who'd frozen in place when they ran inside, her eyes wide with hope and fear at the same time. Colby stood guard, watching over the girl while Max scooped her up in his arms and ran with her outside.

One safe. Two to go.

Dillon gave Donna and Blake a signal to search the west side of the building while he and Chris headed east. Colby and Max would back all of them up, helping where needed and ensuring that no one but Mrs. Grant and her remaining daughter escaped their net.

The building formed a rectangle with rows of six-foot-high cubicle walls, divided in the middle by a line of glassed-in offices, bathrooms and conference rooms. Solid walls acted as fire-breaks every twenty feet. The two teams would have to search and clear each section in a grid pattern before moving to the next.

Blake and Donna had just stepped down one of the aisles when a scratching sound whispered through the wall one aisle over. They both crouched down, as if the move had been choreographed. Which, if he thought about it, had been. All of their training had embedded itself as muscle memory. They worked seamlessly together, each of them knowing what the other was thinking, what they needed to do next. And everything was going like clockwork.

Until now.

Because the next logical step in the plan was for her to wait at one end of the aisle, while he crept to the other end. Then they would converge in a flanking maneuver and confront whoever was in the next aisle. That was their training. That was what they should do.

But he couldn't.

This past week, they'd shared everything a man and woman could share—their hopes, their fears, their minds…their bodies. They'd become one in every sense of the word. And then they'd run down a tunnel to save their friends, a perfect team, and had saved them all.

But he hadn't saved her. He hadn't saved Donna.

It had always been his belief that if they ever got in a tight spot, between her skills and his, the bad guys would have no chance. And that if she ever faltered, he'd be there to protect her, to keep her safe.

But he hadn't been.

That fateful moment during the shoot-out, it had been Lopez—not Blake—who'd made the kill shot that had saved Donna's life. He'd been running on adrenaline ever since, never slowing down enough to process what had happened. But it all caught up to him now, and he knew, he couldn't do it. He couldn't let the woman he loved round that corner, run into the next aisle, into danger. Because he was no longer certain that he could protect her. And that knowledge had his hands shaking, his palms sweating inside his gloves, his vision tunneling down to dark spots.

He couldn't do this.

He couldn't send her into danger and hope that she would be okay. The very idea was insanity.

He just couldn't.

Breathe. Her lips moved, forming the silent word. Her beautiful face wavered in his vision.

Breathe.

His lungs burned.

Breathe.

Air suddenly rushed in. The darkness began to fade. He drew another gulp of air. Then another.

She smiled and gave him the thumbs-up sign.

He tried to smile back but wasn't sure he'd managed more than a grimace.

Everything came into sharp focus now. The scratching noise sounded again, from farther up the aisle. Like fabric scuffing against carpet. Whoever was in the next aisle was moving, crawling. Friend or foe? There was no way to know.

Donna motioned for him to stay. Then she signaled that she would head to the next aisle. Alone.

She crept back a step, toward the mouth of the aisle.

He grabbed her arm, stopping her.

She arched a brow in question.

I love you. He silently mouthed the words.

I know, she mouthed back. Then she grinned and gave him an outrageous wink.

The tightness in his chest eased. He wanted to laugh with joy. He wanted to grab her in his arms and crush her to him, never let her go. But that could wait. It would have to. Because this amazing, smart, strong, capable woman loved him. She'd told him that with actions, if not words. And that gave him the strength to see past his fear, to trust her, trust himself and face whatever might lie ahead.

Because he sure as hell wasn't going to let her face it alone.

He motioned for her to wait, and he crept down the long aisle to the other end. When they were both in position, he held up three fingers, counting down.

Three.

Two.

One.

They both rushed around the wall of cubicles into the next aisle. A young girl, the second daughter, backed up against the wall, her eyes wide with terror.

Blake jerked his gun to the side, while Donna hurried to her and murmured low words, soothing her.

"Second daughter located," Blake whispered into the mic, and gave the location. Moments later, Max was there, scooping the girl up in his arms, while Chris watched over them. Then they were gone, hustling her out of the building.

The mic crackled. Dillon announced that they'd taken down Sanchez's man, who'd been guarding Grant's family. Colby had him handcuffed, with leg shackles to be extra safe, and was taking him out of the building.

"One more bad guy—or bad girl—to go," Dillon announced.

"Maybe, maybe not," Blake warned, having learned from the paint ball exercise. "Be alert. There could be others."

"Noted," Dillon's voice crackled through the mic.

Donna smiled at Blake and made a rolling motion with her hand. Together, as a team, they headed into the next aisle.

In the end, it was Dillon who captured Stacy Bell, without incident. Donna and Blake were there, backing him up. As a team, they surrounded her, took her into custody with no shots fired, and escorted a nearly hysterical Mrs. Grant out of the building, unharmed. As soon as she saw her two daughters waiting near an ambulance, she let out a heartbreaking sob and ran to them. The little family huddled together, crying, but smiling through their tears, because everything was going to be okay.

Chapter Nineteen

Donna leaned against the railing of Chris Downing's back deck, unable to keep from smiling as she watched her fellow SWAT teammates and their wives, all together, once again. Minus Randy, of course. But he would always be there, in their hearts. And his mother, barely a month after Randy's funeral, was with them, too. She'd become a part of their extended family. And she was smiling and seemed to be enjoying herself, at Chris's expense, offering him tips about how to grill the perfect steak, tips Donna was quite certain he didn't want, since he considered himself a master at cooking out.

Over the top of Mrs. Carter's head, Chris gave her a suffering look, silently pleading with her to save him. She grinned and shook her head. Because she knew he didn't really want to be saved. He was a softy inside, like all the big, tough SWAT team members. Besides, if he really needed saving, his wife, Julie, would take care of it. She was inside the kitchen right now, readying some corncobs to put on the grill.

Ashley was on the other side of the grill, bouncing her toddler daughter on her hip, laughing about something Dillon had just whispered in her ear. The man was truly smitten with both his wife and his daughter. Seeing them together always surprised and delighted Donna, because Ashley drew out the joy and laughter, the softness inside Dillon that he normally kept hidden under a tough, macho-guy exterior.

Much like Blake.

She sighed as she watched him near the deck steps, appearing to be truly fascinated by the gardening wisdom of Claire, the chief's wife, as she told him how to grow the biggest, juiciest tomatoes, and how to know if a watermelon was truly ripe and sweet. Then again, maybe he wasn't pretending. It had taken Donna months to see past that brooding, serious, intimidating persona he tended to use as his shield against the world. But now that she did, she realized just how sweet, caring and wonderful he truly was.

Blake Sullivan was a marshmallow inside.

He cared deeply about others, and what they thought. Sometimes he cared a little too much, which had led to him getting hurt too many times. So he had a habit of putting up walls to protect himself, to hide his true emotions, his fears, his insecurities. Which was why he seemed so prickly to those who didn't really get to know him. But once they did, once they were through that wall, the rewards were endless.

Oh, there'd been some rough moments between them, particularly after the rescue operation where they'd saved Grant's family. All those fears and insecurities had reared their ugly head. Blake had suffered his first-ever panic attack inside that building, and had been mortified that she'd been there to witness it. But knowing the reason for it, that he'd been terrified that she might get hurt, had pushed her over the edge she'd been clinging to—that emotional edge, wavering between an intense infatuation and full-blown love. Letting go and falling to the other side had been the best decision she'd ever made.

Of course, they'd both had to report to Dillon that Blake had suffered that panic attack. After all, if it happened once, it could happen again. Which of course could be extremely dangerous for all of them in their line of work. But Dillon was being supportive, because he too had grown to see the value in Blake, as both a member of their team and as a friend. And they would face the difficulties together, and if necessary, make some difficult decisions. Like whether the panic attack was actually part of a larger problem—

PTSD—that Blake had been ignoring since his military days.

His military days.

Turned out, there was a whole lot of baggage buried in his past, baggage he'd only just begun to open up about, in little pieces. Frightening, dark little pieces that made her want to weep for what he'd endured. And gave her a whole new level of understanding for why he'd put up those walls of his and why he was consumed with wanting to protect people, especially her.

Oh, how she loved this man.

He looked over the top of Claire's head and smiled at her. Not the suffering kind of smile Chris had given her, but a true, I'm-loving-talking-to-this-wise-woman kind of smile. He was enjoying life, his new friends, his team. And her.

She smiled back, her heart nearly bursting from joy.

"Get a room, will ya?" Max's wife, Bex, joined her by the railing. "I swear, I've never seen a couple exchange more puppy dog looks between them."

"Uh-huh. Like you and Max aren't sickeningly sweet."

Bex sighed and stared off into the backyard where Max was talking animatedly with Colby and his new wife, Piper. "Love is in the air, I guess. Who'd have thought the entire SWAT team would end up head over heels in love like this? We're all turning into our parents."

"Is that such a bad thing?"

Bex smiled as she watched her own husband. "No, I guess it's not. Hey, did you ever hear the resolution of the FBI's investigation into Grant's actions?"

"I think the investigation is still ongoing. But Grant is cooperating, taking full responsibility for everything that happened. He's so happy to have his family safe and sound, that I don't think he even cares what happens to him."

"It's kind of sad, isn't it?" Bex said. "I'd like to think I wouldn't have done what he did. But, honestly, if Max was in danger, there's probably nothing I wouldn't do, no line I wouldn't cross, if it meant saving his life."

Donna nodded. "I know what you mean. But I'm still not at the forgive-and-forget stage. It still hurts too much. I miss Randy."

"We all do. But the pain will fade in time. Life must go on." Bex kissed her cheek. "I'd better go rescue Piper. She's new to our extended family and looks bored to death over whatever Colby and Max are discussing. I wouldn't want to scare her away. She might not ever come back when Colby comes to visit."

She headed off to save her new friend.

Blake caught Donna's attention and motioned for her to join him. The chief and his wife were over by the grill now, setting up mouthwatering side dishes on a little table, leaving Blake alone. Finally.

She hurried to him, delighted when he leaned down and kissed her full on the lips.

"What was that for?" she breathed, clinging to him.

"Just because."

He checked his watch, which he'd done several times this afternoon. She was about to ask him why he kept checking it when Chris called out that the steaks were ready.

Blake checked his watch again.

"Is something wrong?" she asked, as they moved to the side to let others head up on the deck to get their food.

"Yes and no. I hate to ask, but would you mind skipping the steaks? At least for now. We can come back later. I'm sure Chris will save us some leftovers. There's something I want to show you. And it really can't wait."

Disappointment slashed through her. She'd been thoroughly enjoying the cookout, seeing all her teammates and their families. But the excitement in Blake's tone told her this was important to him. So she smiled and put her hand in his.

"How long will this take?" she asked. "Should I grab my purse from inside?"

"Not long. We can come back and get it." He tugged her with him through the yard, toward the front of the house.

Everyone waved goodbye. None of them seemed surprised that they were leaving.

"Blake? What's going on?" she asked.

"You'll see."

Twenty minutes later, they were on the other side of town, sitting in Blake's truck, just off a two-lane rural highway. Tall oak trees shaded them and partially obscured them from view. A faded billboard sat opposite them on the other side of the road, advertising the best burgers in town at Eva-Marie's Diner on Magnolia Street, catty-corner from the Piggly Wiggly. A claim Donna had to admit was true. They did have the best cheeseburgers she'd ever tasted.

Blake checked his watch again.

"Blake? Will you please tell me why we're here, and why you keep checking your watch?"

"Wait one more minute. Just watch the highway."

She let out a frustrated breath and crossed her arms. The love of her life was trying to bore her to death, if she didn't die of frustration first. "I'm watching. What's going to happen next? Is a chicken going to cross the road? Are we going to find out the answer to the age-old question of why?"

He grinned, then pulled her close and kissed her so deeply, so passionately, that she practically slid into a boneless puddle when he let her go.

Maybe she should complain more often.

She was about to do that very thing, and see if it gained her another kiss, when he straightened in his seat.

"Watch," he said, sounding as excited as a little kid.

A red convertible came into view, barreling down the highway toward them with its top down, obviously going well above the speed limit. As it got closer, Donna recognized the woman at the wheel. The mayor's wife. The same woman who'd sped through a school zone, endangering children. The same woman who'd pushed the mayor into firing both her and Blake when Grant was running things.

"Where's a traffic cop when you need one?" she muttered.

"Funny you should say that."

The car sped past them.

A motorcycle cop zipped out from behind the Eva-Marie Diner billboard and raced down the highway after the little red convertible, lights flashing and siren blaring. A few seconds later, both were pulled over on the side of the road, and the motorcycle cop was walking up to the mayor's wife's car door.

Donna sat bolt upright in her seat. "You didn't."

"I did." He was grinning so hard his cheeks had to hurt. "I asked around, found out she speeds down this road every Sunday, oblivious of anyone else who might be out for a Sunday drive. I figured it might be time to teach her the perils of speeding through Blount County. We don't put up with that stuff around here."

She grinned. "Thank you."

"You're welcome."

This time, she was the one who kissed him. She held nothing back. She told him she loved him in every touch, every slide of her hands through his hair, in the way she clung to him, half on his lap. She didn't think she could ever get enough of him. And the way he kissed her back, she knew he felt the same.

When they broke apart, their breathing choppy, pulses slamming in their veins, he shakily pushed her back onto her side of the seat and fastened her seat belt. His hands were still shaking when he fastened his. He put the truck in Drive and gave her a long, lingering look.

"Do you want to go watch Officer Lynch give the mayor's wife a ticket?"

She slowly shook her head. "I think my vendetta against the mayor's wife is over. She's in my past. You're my future. Take me home, Blake. Take me home to Destiny."

"I love you," he said, his voice husky. "You know that, right?"

She took his hand in hers and rested them together on the seat between them. "I know. I love you, too. Let's get out of here before that cop has to turn around and give us a ticket for indecent exposure." She unbuttoned the top button on her shirt.

Blake's eyes widened. He slammed the gas. The truck peeled out onto the highway, in the opposite direction of the little drama playing out behind them. Donna could practically feel the mayor's wife's glare burning into the back of her head, no doubt knowing exactly who had orchestrated her getting a ticket today. But none of that mattered. Not really.

What mattered was that Donna had wonderful friends and a family that made her life whole.

What mattered was the man beside her, a brave, strong, wonderful man, who understood her, both her strengths and her weaknesses, and reveled in them.

What mattered, above all else, was that no matter how hard life got, she would never be alone. Because she had Blake, the love of her life, her destiny.

* * * * *

Look for more books from award-winning author Lena Diaz later in 2018.

And don't miss the previous books in the TENNESSEE SWAT *miniseries:*

*MOUNTAIN WITNESS
SECRET STALKER
STRANDED WITH THE DETECTIVE*

And the book that started it all, TENNESSEE TAKEDOWN!

Available now from Harlequin Intrigue!

Get 4 FREE REWARDS!

We'll send you 2 FREE Books
plus 2 FREE Mystery Gifts.

Harlequin Presents® books feature a sensational and sophisticated world of international romance where sinfully tempting heroes ignite passion.

FREE
Value Over
$20

YES! Please send me 2 FREE Harlequin Presents® novels and my 2 FREE gifts (gifts are worth about $10 retail). After receiving them, if I don't wish to receive any more books, I can return the shipping statement marked "cancel." If I don't cancel, I will receive 6 brand-new novels every month and be billed just $4.55 each for the regular-print edition or $5.55 each for the larger-print edition in the U.S., or $5.49 each for the regular-print edition or $5.99 each for the larger-print edition In Canada. That's a savings of at least 11% off the cover price! It's quite a bargain! Shipping and handling is just 50¢ per book in the U.S. and 75¢ per book in Canada*. I understand that accepting the 2 free books and gifts places me under no obligation to buy anything. I can always return a shipment and cancel at any time. The free books and gifts are mine to keep no matter what I decide.

Choose one: ☐ **Harlequin Presents®** ☐ **Harlequin Presents®**
　　　　　　　　 Regular-Print 　　　　　　 **Larger-Print**
　　　　　　　　 (106/306 HDN GMYX) 　　　 (176/376 HDN GMYX)

Name (please print)

Address　　　　　　　　　　　　　　　　　　　　　　　　　　　　Apt. #

City　　　　　　　　　　　State/Province　　　　　　　　　Zip/Postal Code

Mail to the Reader Service:
IN U.S.A.: P.O. Box 1341, Buffalo, NY 14240-8531
IN CANADA: P.O. Box 603, Fort Erie, Ontario L2A 5X3

Want to try two free books from another series! Call 1-800-873-8635 or visit www.ReaderService.com.

*Terms and prices subject to change without notice. Prices do not include applicable taxes. Sales tax applicable in N.Y. Canadian residents will be charged applicable taxes. Offer not valid in Quebec. This offer is limited to one order per household. Books received may not be as shown. Not valid for current subscribers to Harlequin Presents books. All orders subject to approval. Credit or debit balances in a customer's account(s) may be offset by any other outstanding balance owed by or to the customer. Please allow 4 to 6 weeks for delivery. Offer available while quantities last.

Your Privacy—The Reader Service is committed to protecting your privacy. Our Privacy Policy is available online at www.ReaderService.com or upon request from the Reader Service. We make a portion of our mailing list available to reputable third parties that offer products we believe may interest you. If you prefer that we not exchange your name with third parties, or if you wish to clarify or modify your communication preferences, please visit us at www.ReaderService.com/consumerschoice or write to us at Reader Service Preference Service, P.O. Box 9062, Buffalo, NY 14240-9062. Include your complete name and address.

HP18

Get 4 FREE REWARDS!

We'll send you 2 FREE Books plus 2 FREE Mystery Gifts.

FREE Value Over $20

Both the **Romance** and **Suspense** collections feature compelling novels written by many of today's best-selling authors.

YES! Please send me 2 FREE novels from the Essential Romance or Essential Suspense Collection and my 2 FREE gifts (gifts are worth about $10 retail). After receiving them, if I don't wish to receive any more books, I can return the shipping statement marked "cancel." If I don't cancel, I will receive 4 brand-new novels every month and be billed just $6.74 each in the U.S. or $7.24 each in Canada. That's a savings of at least 16% off the cover price. It's quite a bargain! Shipping and handling is just 50¢ per book in the U.S. and 75¢ per book in Canada*. I understand that accepting the 2 free books and gifts places me under no obligation to buy anything. I can always return a shipment and cancel at any time. The free books and gifts are mine to keep no matter what I decide.

Choose one: ☐ **Essential Romance**   ☐ **Essential Suspense**
                        (194/394 MDN GMY7)   (191/391 MDN GMY7)

Name (please print)

Address   Apt. #

City   State/Province   Zip/Postal Code

Mail to the **Reader Service:**
IN U.S.A.: P.O. Box 1341, Buffalo, NY 14240-8531
IN CANADA: P.O. Box 603, Fort Erie, Ontario L2A 5X3

Want to try two free books from another series? Call 1-800-873-8635 or visit us at www.ReaderService.com.

*Terms and prices subject to change without notice. Prices do not include applicable taxes. Sales tax applicable in NY. Canadian residents will be charged applicable taxes. Offer not valid in Quebec. This offer is limited to one order per household. Books received may not be as shown. Not valid for current subscribers to the Essential Romance or Essential Suspense Collection. All orders subject to approval. Credit or debit balances in a customer's account(s) may be offset by any other outstanding balance owed by or to the customer. Please allow 4 to 6 weeks for delivery. Offer available while quantities last.

Your Privacy—The Reader Service is committed to protecting your privacy. Our Privacy Policy is available online at www.ReaderService.com or upon request from the Reader Service. We make a portion of our mailing list available to reputable third parties that offer products we believe may interest you. If you prefer that we not exchange your name with third parties, or if you wish to clarify or modify your communication preferences, please visit us at www.ReaderService.com/consumerschoice or write to us at Reader Service Preference Service, P.O. Box 9062, Buffalo, NY 14240-9062. Include your complete name and address.

STRS18

READERSERVICE.COM

Manage your account online!

- Review your order history
- Manage your payments
- Update your address

> *We've designed the*
> *Reader Service website*
> *just for you.*

Enjoy all the features!

- Discover new series available to you, and read excerpts from any series.
- Respond to mailings and special monthly offers.
- Browse the Bonus Bucks catalog and online-only exculsives.
- Share your feedback.

Visit us at:

ReaderService.com